DANCING THROUGH LIFE
BOOK EIGHT

Freedom
DANCE

PATRICIA M. ROBERTSON

Chapter 1

Detroit – Present Day

Letty kicked a path through the room, littered with rags, papers, fast food wrappers, pizza boxes, and other remnants of dinners eaten in haste. She gingerly moved her booted and bandaged foot lest she slip on the rubble. The white of her cast contrasted against her warm brown skin. She lifted her right foot so as not to allow any of the debris to rub against her designer shoe, noticing rat droppings that warned her that live rodents couldn't be that far away.

"The building is sound. We had it inspected." Sara picked up a newspaper and tossed it aside, then wiped her paint-stained white hands on her pants. "It just needs a good cleaning."

Each room shared a similar story. A story of decay. How many homeless men and women have made this place home over the years? Had families gathered here for warmth during cold months? Letty sidestepped a pizza box.

"I saved the best for last," Sara said as she led Letty up a flight of stairs. The bar had not been set too high, Letty thought as she continued to tiptoe around mounds of waste. When they reached the landing of the stairs, Sara unlocked the chains that held double oak doors shut and opened them to display a ballroom. Overhead what appeared to be a chandelier was covered with a protective lining. Though vagrants had invaded the first floor, they had not come as far as the ballroom, it being in the innermost part of the building. There was still some trash in the room, a newspaper here or there, but for the most part it had been left alone.

"The chandelier is intact. We wrapped it to protect it and put the chain on the door to keep the room from any damage. This room was what sold us on the place." Sara's voice echoed through the spacious room.

Letty walked to the middle of the room and stood directly under the chandelier. She saw men and women in Civil War attire dancing about the room, the women in long, flouncy dresses, the men in suits or uniforms. Then she imagined little girls in tutus pirouetting about the floor, laughing and giggling as they danced. She saw herself, barefoot, no longer hampered by a boot, in a sleek, form-fitting leotard and wrap-around skirt, flying across the room, arms high, legs leaping, crinkled dark hair held back from her face with a scarf and flowing down her back. She saw potential.

Letty loved dancing with the dance company of Alvin Ailey, loved New York. The two years studying with Alvin Ailey II and then three years with the actual dance troupe had been a dream come true. But what do you do after you realize a dream? Perhaps she needed a new dream. That was what she told herself. Something was missing. She wasn't sure what. Maybe she would find it here, in her home state. The shelf life of a dancer was limited at best. She would be giving up some of her prime dance years if she joined this venture with Sara and her friends. She wasn't sure why she was even considering it. The right offer at the right time? Or maybe she was just ready for something different, someone different.

"So, what do you think? Are you in?" Sara asked.

Was she in? Was she ready to leave everything for a dream? Was she ready to take a chance on Detroit?

"It will work," she told Sara.

"I knew you would see what I see." Sara hugged Letty. "I've got to pick up my kids, but we'll talk more tonight."

"Will the building be ready in time for fall classes?"

"We can begin cleaning it up this weekend. We were just waiting for your approval before finalizing the deal."

"Let's do this." What was she doing, Letty thought even as she heard the words come out of her mouth?

Chapter 2

Cascade Falls - 1847

Letty lifted the canvas cover and peered out at the sky. Cloud cover. Not a star in sight.

"Always look for the north star," her daddy had told her. "North. That the road to freedom." But now Daddy was gone.

Her twelve-year-old brain replayed the events of the previous night, trying to make sense of it. After so many days of walking by night, hiding and sleeping by day, crossing a river in a boat they found, they thought they had made it. She remembered that boat.

Letty had waited with her family on the shore of the river. This was the biggest river she had ever seen. How were they going to cross? She watched her daddy wade out into waist-deep water. What if the ground give way? What if her daddy drowned? What would they do? In the distance she heard the howls of blood hounds, searching for their prey. Was it them they were after? Her ma had wiped their feet with onions to mask their smell. Maybe it hadn't worked. She watched her daddy wade downstream a mite then motion for them to join him. He had found a small boat. Had it been left for them? By who? They climbed in and glided to freedom.

They had been welcomed in the North by white people no less. Strangers, yet they trusted their life to them. People her daddy and ma didn't know. She sensed her parents' concern. Dare they trust these people? Her daddy talked about a road to freedom, a secret road. You had to travel it by night. There were stations along the way and station managers. They had to find the right ones.

"It a mystery," her daddy had teased her brother Aaron, turning it into a game. Letty knew it was far from a game. "You follow the clues and they lead you to the right places and people. When in doubt, go north."

"How do you know north?" Aaron had asked.

"The brightest star in the sky. See that water dipper? The star at the top. That the north star. And if there no stars, moss grows on the north side of the tree. Feel for moss. When in doubt, go north."

Letty wondered what direction they were headed as they bumped along in the rough-hewn wooden wagon. Five people crowded together. Six minus one, that one being her daddy. The five included her ma, older sister, younger brother, herself and Sarai, a stranger who had become family.

They had no choice but to trust the driver of the wagon. Next to him was a young man, a boy, hardly her age. They exchanged words at times, but for the most part they drove in silence. What if it was a trap? What if he was taking them back south? Letty huddled closer to her sister as the wagon pulled to a stop.

"Here we are," the driver said. A hint of light was seen, coming over the horizon as Letty crawled out from under the canvas along with the rest of the travelers.

"Come inside where it's warm." A white woman with a kind smile came out of a large white farm house to greet and help them climb down. "You must be tired and hungry after your trip." The house was nothing like the mansions of the South. Nothing like the massa's plantation, yet a far cry from the one-room shack that had been their home for so long.

"No, ma'am," her mother answered. "If it all the same to you, we stay in the barn."

"Nonsense. You need a nice hot breakfast and a chance to warm up."

Hot food and a warm kitchen. Sounded like heaven to Letty. She looked at her mother, asking with her eyes.

"Thank you kindly," her mother accepted the offer.

"I heard about what happened in Indiana," the woman said after serving bacon, warm mush with maple syrup and coffee to the group.

The flavors floated on Letty's tongue as she let them linger in her mouth, savoring every hint of seasoning, sweet and smoked. Was this heaven? Was this North? Were they finally going to stop? Three little girls stood in the corner and watched as they ate, the girls' eyes wide with wonder.

"Girls, don't stare. It is not polite," the woman scolded. "Hattie," she called to the oldest. She appeared to be Aaron's age. "Come here. Help me serve our guests. Bring over some more of this porridge for this young man."

Aaron had greedily gulped down his portion of porridge, hoping, but not daring to ask for more.

Being served by white women, Letty didn't know what to think. It somehow didn't seem right. Was it a trap?

"I am so sorry about your husband," the woman said again. Ma didn't answer. What was there to say? The woman continued to try to engage her mother and Sarai in conversation. No, ma'am. Yes, ma'am. Thank you, ma'am, was all they said, as befitted addressing a white woman.

"You must be tired. You can sleep in our spare room."

"No, ma'am. We sleep in the barn," her mother said. "Then tonight we move on."

The driver of the wagon came into the room. Letty had overheard voices outside. "I am afraid it won't be safe to move you tonight. There's word of more bounty hunters coming from down south. You would be safer here in the house with us. We can hide you if anyone comes looking for you. It might not be safe for a few days or more."

Her mother's face was strained and tense, holding back sadness. "We sleep in the barn," she insisted.

"Very well then," the man agreed. "Hattie, get blankets for our guests," he told his daughter. "Be quick about it. Before the sun comes all the way up." The woman put some bread and cheese in a basket and let them out the back door to the barn.

Letty hadn't wanted to leave the warm kitchen, but knew better than to cross her mother. The musty smell of hay and horses assaulted them as they entered the barn. They crawled into the hay loft and set about making a bed for themselves.

"We'll keep a look-out," the man said. "If someone comes, we may need to sneak you back into the main house where we have hiding places."

"Thank you kindly," was her mother's response.

They lay together in the hay as she watched the sun come up through the window in the loft.

"Now it just us," her ma said. "We can talk."

"Ma, what 'bout Daddy?" Abigail asked. "What we gon' do?"

"We gon' do what Daddy wanted us to do, go north, to Canada," Ma said.

"But what 'bout Daddy?" Abigail asked again.

"He a grown man. He can take care of hisself. I have to take care of you," Ma responded.

"That right," Sarai added. "No need to fret 'bout your daddy."

Letty knew she was lying. She didn't know how she knew, she just did. Sometimes she knew these things.

"Get some sleep now," her ma said.

Letty lay quietly next to her sister but she couldn't sleep. The events of the previous night came back to haunt her, kept her tossing and turning.

Chapter 3

Cascade Falls – Present Day

Peter stared at the plate Esther put in front of him. Baked fish with some type of seasoning, a plain baked potato, green beans and a side salad, vinegar and oil dressing, no cheese or croutons. He gave Esther "the look."

"What? Do you want a chicken breast instead?" Esther had an arrangement with the cooks for the retirement community that she and Peter had moved into last spring. After her recovery from her stroke last year, Esther had finally been convinced to give her house to her daughter, Kathleen, and down-size. They had moved in with visions of being free to travel without having to worry about their home. Little had Peter known how soon he would need the benefits of the retirement community. The cooks made chicken breast or fish for him separate from the rest. No breading, no deep frying, no creamy sauce or butter. A few other residents were on the same restrictions. All Esther had to do was go to the kitchen door and ask.

"I don't like green beans," Peter grunted.

"I know, but the cauliflower was drowning in cheese sauce."

"Mmmmm, cheese," Peter murmured. He missed cheese.

"It's not that bad," Esther told him. "There's sugar-free apple crisp for dessert." No sugar, no taste. Peter poured pepper on his potato and poked at it. How he missed butter. On this diet he had lost twenty pounds. But recently he had plateaued. He couldn't lose any more weight no matter what he did.

"Keep at it," the dietician at rehab told him. "Eventually you'll start to lose again, as long as you don't get discouraged and back slide."

"Twenty more pounds and you'll be a new man," his doctor reassured him. "We may be able to take you off of your blood pressure medicine." It had been easy at first. After that scare in June, he had been highly motivated. The pounds were sliding off and he didn't miss his favorite foods. But now, the thought of a lifetime without butter and cheese made him question whether it was worth it.

"Peter, at your next doctor appointment, we'll talk to him about maybe adding a little butter and cheese to your diet," Esther said. Peter hated it when she talked to him like he was a kid who needed to be coaxed to eat his vegetables. When he complained about it, she told him to stop acting like a kid and she'd stop treating him like one.

"We are quite a pair," Esther commented.

"How so?" Peter asked.

"You and me. It's a good thing we have each other."

"No one else would have us."

"Speak for yourself. There's a number of unattached gentlemen here who have their eye on me."

"Well, there are any number of single women here just waiting for a man to cook for. And I bet they wouldn't begrudge him a bit of butter now and then." Esther laughed and put her hand on his.

"It's okay, Peter. You took care of me, now I take care of you. We take care of each other. That's what marriage is about." Peter had taken care of Esther after her stroke last year. In comparison, this was nothing. Still it was good they had moved into this retirement community when they had.

"Moving here was the best decision we made," Peter said. "Second only to marrying you," he added.

"You better not forget that," Esther told him. He knew she appreciated his care for her last year. He appreciated what she was doing for him. If only it didn't feel like such a trap.

"I sometimes think it would be better to live my life the way I want, eat what I want. What good is life if you can't enjoy it?"

"It will get better, Peter," Esther assured him.

"Will it?"

It had all started that morning two days into their Alaskan cruise. All Peter remembered was a crushing pain in his chest and feeling like he couldn't breathe. Fortunately, they had not been far out of port. The ship medic had come immediately and he had been life-flighted by helicopter to a hospital in Anchorage. After a series of tests, it was ruled a mild heart attack.

"It's good you received help right away. There appears to be little damage to your heart," the doctor told him. They kept him overnight for observation. He was given a list of food and drink to avoid: alcohol, red meat, cheese, butter and other rich foods. Everything he loved. He was to report to his doctor for a follow up when they got home. They released him after two days with warnings to avoid strenuous exercise or stress.

"Doctor, we're on a cruise," Peter told him. "I don't know how I can be under any less stress. I'll just be sitting on the deck and watching the world go by."

"Good, but watch those buffets. And have the ship medic monitor your blood pressure every day."

They had been able to meet up with their cruise at their next port of call and finished out the trip, but it wasn't the same. Peter knew Esther was on edge, watching him for any sign of another heart attack. He was on edge too. The cruise couldn't get over soon enough so he could get home to his own doctor. He ate sparingly from the abundance of food and allowed himself only one glass of wine each night. Even that was taken from him when he got home.

There was no need for a stent or any surgical procedure. He just needed to watch what he ate, lose weight and start an exercise program.

"In a year, you'll be a new man," the doctor assured him.

"I kind of liked the man he was," Esther teased. "I'm pretty attached to this old man." She placed her arm around him and squeezed. "We'll do whatever it takes to keep him around. Would hate to have to break in a new model."

Hardly three months into it and he was ready to give it all up. What good was life if you weren't able to enjoy it?

Chapter 4

Cascade Falls – Present Day

Kathleen clicked off her phone with a sigh and looked across the dinner table at Joe. It had not taken long for them to make her mom's home their home. It was as if that brief stay in the manse had been a prelude to something better. She knew she was at home, sitting at the same table she had sat at for years, in the home she had grown up in, sharing it with her new husband. Now, if only Stephanie would get her life together.

"Something wrong?" Joe asked.

"Stephanie. I think something's wrong, but she won't let on what. Quit worrying, she keeps saying. How can I not worry?" They had come a long way since that afternoon in June when Stephanie, Joe's errant daughter, had announced she was pregnant. Somehow, she and Stephanie, her new step-daughter, had found a way to connect in ways they hadn't been able to before. A blessing, she guessed. Too bad it took an unplanned pregnancy to do it.

"Did you remind her she can move in with us till the baby was born?" Joe asked.

"Yes. The answer's the same. She's determined to handle this on her own."

Kathleen remembered that day in June far too well.

"How far along are you?" she had asked Stephanie after the announcement.

"Two or three months, I think."

"You think, you think. Since when did you think about anything," Joe exploded. This was a side of her husband, the pastor, she had not yet seen. But if anyone could get Joe to lose his pastoral cool, it was Stephanie.

"It's okay, Joe. I've got this." Kathleen had put her hand on his arm to calm him down.

"Do you know who the father is?" Joe asked, ignoring her.

"Of course, Dad. I'm not that bad," Stephanie retorted. "Or at least, I think I know. I knew you would think the worst."

"You think you know?" Joe walked away, put his hand on his head then turned back around. "Does the father know?"

"I told you, I think I know who the father is, but he doesn't need to know."

"I think he has some part to play in this."

"I can still get rid of the baby," Stephanie placed her hands on her hips, taunting her father.

"Oh, Stephanie, no," Kathleen went over to Stephanie and put her arm around her. "You don't want to do that."

"How do you know?" Stephanie pulled away from her. "You're not my mother."

"But I know something about having a baby when you aren't married, aren't ready to have a baby. Just think, if I had done that, there would be no Josh or Scott." Stephanie was aware of the situation around Josh and Scott's births. It was no secret, though not usually talked about.

"You need to find out who the father is and contact him," Joe stepped back in.

"You don't know what I need, Dad. If you did you wouldn't be saying that. I don't know what I want to do. I know it was a mistake to tell you, but Josh insisted. Said I had to tell you."

"Josh knows?" Kathleen asked. Josh, her oldest son, and Stephanie had been close since high school.

"He's not the father?" Joe asked.

"No, Dad. He's like my brother. How can you even ask that?"

"Because where you are concerned, Stephanie, I never know what to think."

"We all need some time to cool off. Let's go home and talk about this later," Kathleen stepped between them.

"What are you going to do?" again Joe ignored Kathleen.

"I don't know. I don't know, Dad. Maybe give the baby up for adoption. What do I know about being a parent?" Stephanie turned away to hide her tears.

"What do any of us know?" Joe walked over to her and wrapped his arms around her. "It's okay, Stephie. We'll get through this. We'll figure it out."

"No, Dad. It's my problem and I'll figure it out."

Stephanie had gone back to work the next day.

"You can stay here with us if you want," Kathleen had told her before she left. "If you need time to think about it. Any time. Just call us."

"Thanks, Kathleen, Dad. I do appreciate that. But I've got a job to get back to. I don't want to lose it. I'll call you," she had assured them, then didn't call, as was her custom.

"What was that girl thinking?" Joe had asked after she left.

"I doubt that she was thinking at all. At least the fact that she told us about it, that's a good sign. It means she won't have an abortion, right?"

"I don't know what to think where that girl is concerned."

"I think if she had been planning on getting an abortion, she would have done it before this and not told us. She wouldn't have waited this long, would she?"

"Let's hope for that." Joe hugged her. "What do you think about becoming a grandmother?"

"I don't know. I guess I'll get used to the idea." And that she did. Over the past few months she had more than gotten used to the idea. She was quietly excited about the prospect but tried not to let Stephanie know lest she scare her off and destroy the fragile bond they had formed.

Stephanie still refused to let them know who the father was and continued to talk about giving the baby up for adoption. As far as Kathleen could tell, the only person she talked to was Josh. He was the one who accompanied her to doctor visits and Lamaze classes.

Stephanie refused to learn the baby's gender, refused to get excited. She did what she needed to do to assure the baby's health — no drinking, taking the mega vitamins prescribed by her doctor — but no more than that. It appeared she was just biding her time till the delivery when she would be able to start her life again from where she had left off. As far as Kathleen could tell, the baby was just a blip along the way.

So like her at Stephanie's age. The thought was no comfort to her.

Chapter 5

Detroit – Present Day

What had she done? Sleep was hard to come by as Letty tossed and turned, her mind churning along with her stomach. Was she really going to leave Alvin Ailey for this? For a run-down house in the city of Detroit? She could change her mind, couldn't she? She hadn't signed a contract or anything. She would just tell Sara in the morning.

She was staying in the apartment over Sara's garage while visiting. If she decided to move to Detroit, it would be hers to live in, rent-free, until she could find a place of her own. She appreciated the kindness but was finding it hard to make the decision. She missed New York already, missed her apartment, missed her friends. Why had she come here? Why should she leave New York?

She had been warned about James when she first started dancing with Alvin Ailey.

"He's a high roller. Likes to chase after all the new dancers at Alvin Ailey. Best to watch out for him."

She had watched out for him, and watched him watching her. She had seen him glancing her way, giving her that big grin and flirtatious smile after her first performance, even as he gave a bouquet of flowers to the lead dancer. She should have known better. He continued the flirtation, smiling at her, his white teeth glistening against his dark skin, touching his hand to his forehead in a slight wave whenever he saw her.

"You're Leticia," he stated, sidling next to her as she waited in the crowded club after a performance.

"And you're James," she responded, refusing to look at him.

"How do you know me?"

"Your reputation precedes you." Letty glanced about the club for the other members of the troupe that she was meeting there.

"I hope it was all good."

"It was good all right." Letty saw Shaunte waving to her. "Now if you'll excuse me," she waved back at her friend and tried to push past him.

"See you again, my Midwest girl," James said as he stepped aside just enough to let her pass.

How could she resist? He had lavished flowers and attention on her until she agreed to go out with him. It had been a whirlwind, leaving her heart broken when he chased after a new batch of dancers.

"Consider it a rite of passage," Shaunte had advised her. "Dancers, especially young ones, always have suitors plying them with flowers and praise. It rarely lasts. Enjoy it while you can, then move on."

Shaunte had been dancing with Alvin Ailey for two years longer than her. A fellow Michigander, she had taken on the role of mentor to Letty, teaching her the ropes, everything she didn't learn in dance classes or rehearsals. Shaunte had been the one to warn her about James and the one to help her pick up the pieces afterwards. Letty didn't want to be someone's conquest and so had steeled herself against flowers and smiles, until James came back.

"Baby, I was wrong. You're the one for me. Only you." He had convinced her one time with that line. It wasn't going to work anymore. The only way to be safe from his charms was to go far away. But that hadn't been the only reason for her leaving. She wanted to do more with her life than just dance. Much as she loved dancing, she wanted more.

So, when Sara came along with the proposal of opening a Dance Studio in an abandoned building in Detroit, she didn't exactly jump at the idea, but the thought took up residence in her brain until it grew into a decision. The broken bone in her foot was just the excuse she needed to explore other options.

"It'll be a chance to do in Detroit what you did with Joy's Center for the Arts," Sara told her.

Letty had been instrumental in keeping Joy's Dance Studio open by creating a non-profit Center for the Arts in her home town of Cascade Falls. Her vision had been to provide the arts to children of all ages and socio-economic backgrounds. After helping set up the center, she had received the opportunity to dance with Alvin Ailey II and eventually was accepted into the Alvin Ailey Dance Troupe, a dream come true. At twenty-seven, Letty wasn't ready to call it quits with dreams or dancing, but she was ready for something more.

Sara had been meeting with a random group of artists for several years. They had met through classes and art shows at the Detroit Institute for the Arts. All agreed that struggling artists needed more, a safe place to work their craft, hone their skills. A place open to new ideas and new artists, giving them the opportunity to display their work without having to put a lot of money down. A place for a free exchange of ideas.

The plan was to anchor the center with a dance studio. That's where Letty came in, or so Sara had explained. Letty had been rehearsing for their evening performance when the call came.

"I can't talk now," she told Sara. "Maybe tomorrow morning. Call me tomorrow morning. Then we can talk."

Sara had called. They had talked. Letty put her off again. "Call me when you have a building," she had told Sara. That was three months ago. Then she had come down wrong on her foot during practice, crashing to the floor. The break required that she stay off her foot while it healed, so she had returned home to rest at her parents' home in Cascade Falls, an hour and a half drive from Detroit. That had been fine, until it wasn't. Now, here she was, contemplating a building full of clutter and debris in a city filled with clutter and debris and … potential.

"Detroit could use a dance studio like Alvin Ailey. You could be an extension of Alvin Ailey – Alvin Ailey Detroit. Come on, Letty. What do you say?"

Alvin Ailey Detroit? No way. That was not her, but she found herself agreeing anyway.

"I'll do it. But not as an extension of Alvin Ailey. If I do this, I want it to be my studio."

"Under a board of directors."

"That's right. But I have artistic freedom, right?"

"You won't regret it. You'll love it here," Sara assured her. "Oh, by the way. The house we are buying, it's historical. That's why we are getting it from the city for such a great price. We just have to restore it."

"What's its history?"

"It was part of the Underground Railroad. Beyond that, I'm not sure. I don't know a lot. We'll be researching its history, but for now, we are calling it 'Freedom Home.'" Letty extended her leave of absence from Alvin Ailey in order to explore this option. If it didn't work out, she wanted an escape plan.

Chapter 6

Detroit – Present Day

Letty walked amid the crew of workers cleaning up the debris throughout the building. This was the easy part, clearing up surface clutter. They hauled out bags of debris, then mopped and polished the floors, swept and shampooed the carpets, wiped down the walls, cleaned the banister rails.

"See. I told you we'd have it good as new before the fall," Sara told her.

"I wish it were that simple. … Who's that?" Letty watched a man with a clipboard walking about the building, jotting down notes, then lodging his pencil in his ear where it stood out against his white face.

"That's Derrick, the architect. Remember, I told you about him. He's on our board."

"Oh, he is?"

"Yes, how else would we be able to afford to get this building up to code and within historical guidelines? He's preparing architectural drawings, checking structural soundness, what walls are load bearing, all that stuff for free. Be nice to him."

"Like I'm ever not nice," Letty responded.

"No, I mean it. He can be kind of gruff. Don't let it bother you. This building, it was owned by his grandparents. His parents hadn't been able to, or weren't interested, in keeping it up. They moved out of the area. It fell into disrepair and became city property for back taxes. Derrick has since moved back into the area. He wanted to see the building preserved and we were looking for a space."

"A match made in heaven."

"Some say so. Come on. I'll introduce you." Letty limped over to the man, Sara leading the way. He stood out in his dress slacks, shirt and tie amidst workers in jeans and t-shirts. His brown hair was clipped short and stood up when he ran his hand through it.

"Do you always wear dress clothes to clean up abandoned buildings?" Letty inquired.

"Letty," Sara scolded. "Letty," her voice softened, "this is Derrick Jacobson, the architect and board member I told you about." She turned to Derrick, "Derrick, this is Leticia Anderson. She's going to be opening the dance studio."

"If you can have it ready in time," Letty added.

"Letty used to dance with Alvin Ailey in New York. Remember, Derrick? From our board meetings?" Sara added.

"Oh," he made another notation on his clipboard then shifted the board and pencil to his left hand, leaving his right hand free to shake Letty's hand. "Pleased to meet you," he said.

"Will it?"

"Will it what?"

"Will it be done in time? I want to open by September."

"I don't see why not, unless, of course, we run into a problem."

"What kind of problem?"

"There's always problems when you are dealing with an old building, trying to bring it up to code and still maintain historical integrity. And then there's dealing with the city. Always problems there."

"But can you do it?" Letty asked.

"Yes, but there's papers to be filed. We have to schedule inspections." Derrick continued to jot down notes on his clipboard.

"I thought you had already filed all the paperwork ... haven't you?" Letty turned to Sara.

Derrick answered. "That was just to purchase the building and for preliminary work. There's so much more to be done. My initial assessment of the building was that it was structurally sound but we need to get the electrical system checked and brought up to code, and then the plumbing. Who knows how much damage those vagrants did while living here. All of that has to be taken care of."

"But you will get it done?" Letty asked.

"We'll see," he said. "By the way. I'm dressed like this because I have another meeting after I leave here. Besides, I'm here in my official capacity as architect."

"Oh." Letty had thought he hadn't heard her, so engrossed had he been in his work.

"Here's my card if you have any more questions." He handed Letty his card and excused himself.

"He's a bit of an odd duck," Letty commented after he left.

"He's a board member, Letty. You have to be able to work with him."

"But he is an odd duck, admit it."

"Okay, I admit it." Sara released the smile she had been holding back.

"And I can work with him," Letty assured her. She had worked with worse. What would be so hard about working with an oddball architect?

Chapter 7

Kentucky to Michigan - 1847

Nathaniel stepped forward and boldly waved his hand.

"Ferry ahoy!" he shouted. He knew he had to exude a confidence he didn't have. But he was good at masking his feelings. Years of working in his master's home had taught him well.

At twenty-two he had spent the last twenty years of his life working, first in the fields once he was able to walk, then as a barber in his master's home. With his nimble fingers he had quickly picked up skills and was taught how to cut hair and shave whiskers, sliding a sharp blade under chins, along cheeks, leaving behind a smooth surface. He had learned to keep his mouth shut and ears open. His proximity to white men introduced him to their ways.

As a barber, he had made himself valuable to his master. It always struck him as funny how the white man who beat his slaves, would then entrust his life to the same slaves as he exposed his throat to the blade. Often the master would talk to him like a confidant, telling Nathaniel his secrets, revealing his life to this slave as a counselor. Other times he talked to other men as if Nathaniel wasn't there. Nathaniel listened and played dumb, all the while learning and thinking.

"We will be shipping slaves off to the auction tomorrow, Abe," he told his head overseer.

"How many?"

"What do you think? Old Joe, he is not much good anymore, not since he broke his leg and it never healed properly. And Samson. He has been nothing but trouble. See how he likes it further south. He will be regretting the day he spoke back to me." Nathaniel bit his tongue. Old Joe, he had a family, wife and two kids. Joe's oldest sons had already been sold down south. What would happen to the rest of his family when he was gone? And Samson, he was ornery. Didn't know better than to talk back to white men. Nathaniel had tried to talk to him, but it had been no use.

"What about the women?"

"I imagine we can spare a few. I will talk to the missus about it tonight and let you know tomorrow." No one was safe, not even him. Nathaniel knew that. For the right offer, the master would sell his own soul, probably already had.

That night, he told the others what he had heard. Samson determined to make the break for freedom along with his brother. Old Joe determined to go too, taking his family with him.

"It not safe if I leave without them," he had told Nathaniel.

"But how you manage the journey?" Nathaniel pointed at Joe's leg.

"That," Joe grinned at Nathaniel. "I have the overseer fooled. My leg been healed this past month. Mattie and me, we plan this for some time. He never expect a lame slave to make a run for it. If not tonight, within the fortnight, we gone."

Nathaniel decided to leave too. No telling what the master would do after the others escaped. Might figure out who had warned them. He was travelling alone. Safer that way. He took his big metal scissors for cutting hair, a few coins he had managed to save, cheese and bread his mother had given him for the journey, and wrapped them in a wool blanket formed into a knapsack.

"Now go," his mother hurried him out the door, lest he change his mind. "Don't you worry none 'bout me. I sleep better knowin' you free."

Nathaniel didn't know what to say. Would he ever see her again? Would she be all right after he left? How could he leave her behind?

"Just go. Don't look back. Just keep goin'."

Nathaniel took off through the woods. Word of the escape must have spread quickly throughout the plantation. He could hear the howl of dogs chasing their prey. He knew who that prey was. He couldn't think about the others, couldn't think about those he left behind. He ran till he fell into the muck around a river. What to do? Swimming lessons had not been part of his, or any slave's, education. Better to drown here than go back to the punishment he knew would await him. He waded as far as he dared. The howls grew closer. He couldn't allow himself to feel the fear that was tightening his chest, making his breath come out in shallow gasps. This was no time for fear. He gazed up into the sky, looking for a sign, some sign from God. No sign.

Then the cloud cover broke and he saw a canoe, upstream, by the side of the river. He waded to the canoe, climbed in and paddled across, gliding swiftly and silently lest he draw any attention to himself. On the other side, he jumped off and continued to run, not waiting to listen to the sound of hounds as they reached the edge of the river. His scent was lost in the water. He was safe, for now.

That had been days ago. As he gazed across the Ohio River from Kentucky, he wondered, was it all for naught? How was he going to cross this massive body of water? This was the last ferry over the Ohio. The sun was lowering in the sky. If he didn't take this ferry, he would lose twelve hours of night. He looked down at his feet, clad in the shoes that had been provided him as a house servant. Despite his nights of running through brush and swamps, his clothes were still respectable. He would have to pass as a free man.

"How much?" he asked as the ferry turned back to where he stood.

"A bit," the man answered.

Nathaniel pulled out a ten-cent coin and handed it to the man. "I will pass again. You can make it right when I do," he told the man who happily accepted the bribe.

A white man and colored man were already seated in the ferry.

"You a free man?" the colored man asked.

The white man cuffed him cross the side of his head. "What did you ask that for? Do you think a runaway would dress like him?"

"No, sir," the colored man shook his head and looked down.

Free man? So, is this what it is like to be a free man? Able to come and go as he pleased. Soon he wouldn't just be acting the part, he told himself as the ferry glided over the river. He landed in Ohio, a free man on free soil, but didn't dare stop long to relish the feeling. He knew safety lay further north. He was far too close to the south to let down his guard. He'd heard of bounty hunters chasing escaped slaves through the north. No, he wasn't safe yet.

Nathaniel travelled only at night, sleeping in the woods during the day, foraging for food. After several more nights he came to a village where he thought he saw a black man cutting a log into planks. He appeared to be free. Was it possible? Nathaniel approached him. The man put down his saw, wiped his brow, looked sideways at him and said, "Some folk, they think you get here and you free." He stretched his arms and prepared to pick up the saw again. "But if'n you don't have papers, I wouldn't stay here. There a boarding house up the road a ways in the next town over. They take special guests."

Nathaniel started to thank him but the man was already back at his work as if he hadn't stopped to talk at all. Nathaniel heeded his warning and continued north to the next village. He waited till dark before approaching the boarding house. He still had a few cents in his pack. He would pay for a meal if nothing else. He knocked on the door. It was opened by a white woman with a shawl wrapped around her shoulders.

"I hear you take special guests," he said. The woman looked him over, then glanced about in the night before taking him in.

"Yes. We do," she said. Nathaniel had found the Underground Railroad.

Some forty or more days later, after being cramped into tight spaces in wagons and bounced along bumpy roads in the night, Nathaniel decided it was time for a break, time to stretch his legs a might. He decided to go it alone, walking through Michigan's forests and over its hills.

"When you get to Cascade County, ask for a man named Whitcomb. He can be trusted," the last agent on the railroad told him. He continued north till he came to a land of lakes, rivers and rolling hills. He waded into the lakes, cooling his aching feet, then splashed his face. He rounded the top of a hill and saw below him a small bustling town. He was tired of running. He had come home.

Chapter 8

Cascade Falls – Present Day

Letty lay in her bed in Cascade Falls, listening to the sound of a train whistle coming from somewhere in the dark. Why didn't she remember hearing this before? Maybe she had been too tired to be awakened by the sound.

She remembered learning about the Underground Railroad as a child, in fifth grade. She remembered rushing home after receiving the assignment to research the Underground Railroad in Cascade Falls and being disappointed when she learned it wasn't a magic train like in the Harry Potter books, or even a railroad.

"It's not a railroad at all. It's just people taking slaves in wagons and buggies and hiding them in their homes," she had said at dinner when her father asked what she had learned at school.

"That's better than an actual train, better than magic," her dad told her. "People risked their lives and livelihoods to help the slaves, for something they believed in. That's pretty powerful. Better than any made-up magical train. It's real."

"You think so, Daddy?" Letty asked.

"I know so. It took a lot of courage to accept slaves into your home back then. If you were caught you could have gone to jail."

"What about the slaves?" her brother Jerome joined the conversation. "What about the risks they took? They risked everything. If they were caught, they were brought back and beaten, maimed or killed."

"That's right," her dad said. "They risked everything for freedom. Some things in this world are worth fighting for, worth taking risks for. I'm glad Ms. Simpson teaches about the Underground Railroad every year."

"We're going on a field trip Thursday to see a home that was part of the Underground Railroad," Letty had said.

"That's Ms. Simpson's aunt and uncle's home. Her great grandparents were part of the Underground Railroad. Your ancestors came to Cascade Falls via the Underground Railroad. There were a number of stops in Cascade County. You'll learn about them," he had assured her, and she had. Then she had forgotten about the stories as more important aspects of life as a pre-teen took precedent. Now she searched her mind for those stories.

She continued to lay awake in the pre-dawn darkness, dreading getting up and facing more questions. She had come to her hometown to see her doctor. After the initial doctor visit in New York, Letty had decided it would be easier to convalesce at home under the care of a local podiatrist. She had chosen to stay with this doctor after she moved to Detroit. The drive from Detroit to Cascade Falls wasn't that long, just an hour and a half. It was worth having to deal with her mom if it meant getting this boot off. She wriggled her toes under the covers. She couldn't wait to start dancing again.

"I just don't understand why you have to go to Detroit. There are plenty of needy people here. You could work at Joy's Dance Studio, try out your fancy ideas there instead of Detroit," her mom kept saying.

The more her mom questioned her, the more Letty knew she had made the right decision in not moving back to Cascade Falls.

"Leticia, it's enough that you insisted on moving to New York and dancing with Alvin Ailey. Now it's time to settle down, do something more sensible. Not follow some dream to Detroit."

"It's good to see you too, Mom." Letty hugged her mom, kissed her on her cheek, then proceeded to ignore what she was saying.

"Cliff, you talk to your daughter," her mother told her father.

"Good to have you home, sweetie. How long you staying?" her dad asked.

"That's not what I meant, and you know it."

Letty knew she couldn't postpone the inevitable conversation forever, but for now, she burrowed deeper into the covers, ignoring the sound of her bedroom door opening.

"Leticia, breakfast is ready."

"I don't eat breakfast, Mom. You know that. Just coffee and a piece of dry toast."

"While you are under my roof, you will eat breakfast. Now get up and come down stairs."

Letty sighed and rolled over. "Okay. Just give me a few minutes."

"Fifteen minutes. If you're not up by then, I'm bringing a pan of water."

Letty knew not to take this threat lightly. When her brother Jerome had been in high school, her mother would routinely pull back his covers and throw cold water on his face till he got up. She got out of bed, pulled on a bathrobe and headed downstairs.

"What's on the agenda for today?" her mother asked over breakfast.

"Doctor appointment. Then going to the dance studio, hanging out with Chloe." Chloe had taken over running the dance studio when Letty left. They had remained in touch over the years, Letty giving Chloe pointers and sharing what she was learning at Alvin Ailey. Chloe, with her red-hair and Irish step dancing, was the stable voice from her past, connecting her to Joy's Dance Studio.

"Well, you be home for dinner."

"I was going out with friends."

"You can go out after dinner. Dinner will be at six." Letty decided this wasn't a battle worth fighting. What was it this time?

Letty sighed as she met another young man from her parents' church. Would her mother ever stop the parade of eligible bachelors? Letty made it through dinner then escaped, slipping out by seven to meet Chloe.

She pulled up a chair outside the main classroom of the dance studio looking through the glass at the students. From where she sat, she could watch Chloe put her dancers through their paces while massaging her newly freed foot. What she had heard was true: Ashley was doing much better. There was a marked improvement from last winter.

"Letty, and minus your boot," Kathleen, the director of the Center, joined her.

"Yes, the doctor took it off, though I still need to wear it for a few hours a day or if my foot starts to hurt."

"When will you be able to teach for us again?"

Letty laughed at this. Last year she had agreed to teach a lyrical dance class. "Not this year, I'm afraid, or any time soon. You heard I'm starting my own dance studio in Detroit, didn't you?"

"Yes, our loss. Detroit's gain. You sure I can't convince you to teach here?"

"Have you been talking to my mother?" Letty shook her head and smiled. "I think I have all I can handle with the dance studio in Detroit."

"Just saying, if you change your mind …"

Letty smiled as she heard another familiar voice – Kathleen's mother, Esther.

"Letty, so good to see you again," Esther said. Letty noted her cane. Esther was getting around much better than when she had last seen her. Her husband, Peter, followed behind her.

"Here's the bookkeeping. All up-to-date." Esther handed a packet to Kathleen.

"How are you doing?" Letty asked Peter. "It's good to see you out and about." Her mother kept her up-to-date on what was happening in her hometown, especially her friends from the dance studio. She had heard about Peter's heart attack.

"My jailer lets me out now and then," Peter joked.

"As ornery as ever," Esther added.

"Nothing a cheeseburger wouldn't cure," Peter said.

"Over my dead body," Esther responded.

Peter paused as if considering the idea. Esther poked him playfully in his stomach.

"Clearly he's feeling better. He's feeling good enough to fight with my mom," Kathleen said.

Letty laughed. Joy and her family had been a second family to her while growing up. It was good to be here. Felt like a bit of home.

Letty slipped into a classroom that wasn't being used and stretched while waiting for Chloe.

"You're right," Letty said as Chloe joined her. "Ashley has improved."

"All Ashley is serious about anymore is dancing."

"Really? What brought about this change?"

"I think it had something to do with what Simon Cowell said to her at the America's Got Talent audition last year. Whatever he said, she's either taken it to heart, or she's trying to prove him wrong. Either way, I just know this year she has been more focused than ever before."

"Wouldn't have anything to do with my being so hard on her last winter?" Ashley had attended the course on lyrical dance that Letty had taught last year.

"That too. Hard to say. When she isn't dancing herself, she's helping out in the younger classes, though she's not the best teacher."

"I would have guessed as much. Too impatient and demanding."

"Enough talk about the dance studio," Chloe said. "I didn't get a babysitter to talk dance. We going to your Uncle Delbert's?"

"Always," Letty said. After dinner with her mom, she needed a night out and Uncle Delbert's club was just the place.

Chapter 9

Detroit – Present Day

Once the initial rubble had been cleaned up, there was steady if slow progress on getting the building ready. Broken windows were replaced, the heating system updated, plumbing and wiring all brought up to code. Letty began to believe this was actually going to happen. She worked with Sara on logos for the house and for her school of dance. They came up with designs for flyers and prepared to send them out to prospective students and more importantly, parents of prospective students.

"What's the name of that building?" Letty's mom asked when she called Letty.

"Freedom House. At least that's what we are planning on calling it."

"Then would your dance school be Freedom School of Dance, or Letty's School of Dance …?"

"Or, Letty's Freedom School of Dance?" Letty suggested.

"No, don't like it. Too cumbersome. Freedom School. I like that. Why that name?"

"Because of the building's history as part of the Underground Railroad," Letty explained.

"Really? You know that's how your great grandparents came to Cascade Falls. Through the Underground Railroad. They were runaway slaves."

"What Black person in America doesn't have a tie to the railroad?"

"I'm just saying, it's an interesting story if you ever care to hear it."

"Okay. You've got me. Let me hear it."

"Oh no, I'm not the one to tell it. You've got to hear it from your great aunt Leticia."

"Great Aunt Leticia, my namesake?"

"The same."

"I thought she died years ago."

"No, she just dropped off your radar when you moved to New York. She's alive, though not doing so well. She's in a nursing home in Detroit. As long as you insist on living in Detroit, I wish you would look in on her now and then."

"Sure, Mom." She should have seen this coming. Should have realized her mom had something in mind, some way of getting her to do what she wanted her to do. Still, she was her great aunt, her namesake. "Why didn't you tell me sooner?"

"Well, because, it may not be easy. Visiting her that is."

"Why?" Letty asked.

"You'll see," was all her mom said before ending the conversation.

Letty double-checked the address she had written down for her aunt's nursing home: TLC – Tender Loving Care Rest Home. The neighborhood was not what she had expected, run-down houses, some building shells from fires, others occupied with piles of debris and broken-down cars in the front yard. It was as if someone had taken the bags of debris from Freedom House and dumped them here.

She was grateful when she turned down another street and saw rows of homes, neatly kept up. Nothing luxurious. Simple family dwellings. At the end of the street was a dead end with the nursing home. It, too, was nothing luxurious, showed years of decay, but the yard was clean and tended with flowers. Baskets with mums greeted you at the doorway. As you walked in there was a hominess about the place that felt welcoming. Residents sat in wheelchairs in the lobby, watching guests come and go. Some tried to strike up a conversation, others cried for help.

"Are you Kayla? I'm watching for my granddaughter, Kayla. She's going to take me home," an elderly woman stopped here. She grabbed Letty's hand and pulled her close.

Letty gently pulled her hand away. "I'm sorry. I'm not your granddaughter. I'm sure she will come."

"That's what they all say." The woman pulled her hand back.

"Could I help you?" a woman dressed in slacks and a sweater asked her. Letty noticed a badge pinned to the sweater.

"Yes, I'm looking for my aunt, Leticia Burke."

"You must be Letty. Mrs. Burke is looking forward to your visit. If you'll just sign in, I'll take you to her room." The woman led Letty to the front desk where there was a sign-in registry.

"I'm Vicky Taylor, the social worker here. Mrs. Burke hasn't had many visitors. She'll be happy to see you."

"What about her daughter and her grandkids?"

"I've been here three years. Haven't met any of them. You're the first relative to visit that I know of."

Not even her mother? She thought her mother had visited. "My mother said she comes here now and then, Alicia Anderson?"

"Is that your mom? I have a vague recollection of her coming, but we have so many residents. It's hard to keep track of all of their relatives." Vicky opened a door and walked in with Letty behind her.

"Mrs. Burke, your company has come." There was the distinct odor of urine permeating the room. Aunt Letty was in the bathroom. "Oh, dear. Mrs. Burke, do you need some help? I'll get someone." She turned to Letty. "You can wait in the hall while an aide gets this taken care of, if you don't mind."

"No, that's fine." Letty was happy for any excuse to keep from having to go into that room. Now what had she gotten herself into? She wandered up and down the hallway as staff came and went from her aunt's room. Doors were decorated with wreaths and pictures, anything to make the place more like home. Some of the rooms appeared no bigger than a walk-in closet, with a bathroom attached. Her aunt's room was bigger, had a small living area and bedroom.

When she saw staff leaving her aunt's room, she wandered back in that direction.

"Mrs. Burke, your niece is here. Did you want to talk here or go into the common area?" Vicky motioned for Letty to come closer.

"We'll have more room in the common area," her aunt replied. The social worker wheeled her to the room. "Put me over there by the birds," her aunt instructed. "What about afternoon snack?"

"Someone will bring it soon. Would you like something to drink?" she asked Letty. "Coffee, hot tea?"

"No, thank you. I'm fine."

"Enjoy your visit. Let any of the staff know if you need help," Vicky said as she left.

Letty wasn't sure where to begin. Her aunt had hardly acknowledged her presence. She remembered Aunt Letty had been her favorite aunt at one time, not just because she was named after her. They had been "kindred spirits" as her aunt had always said. What had happened to her?

"Aunt Letty?" She pulled up a chair alongside of her aunt's wheelchair. "Aunt Letty? It's me, Letty. Remember? Letty?"

"Yes, I remember you. You don't have to repeat yourself. Why does everyone treat me like I'm deaf or daft? I don't know which is worse."

"It's good to see you, Aunt Letty."

"Don't lie, child. It's not becoming. If it's so good to see me, how come you took so long to come?"

"I'm sorry, Aunt Letty. I've been in New York. I was a dancer with Alvin Ailey. Do you know them?"

"Of course, I know them. I saw them when they first toured Detroit, before they made a name for themselves and became so uppity." Letty wasn't sure what to say after that. She was grateful for the birds as it gave her something to focus on besides her aunt.

"Did you bring me anything?" Aunt Letty asked.

"No. I'm sorry. I didn't know what to bring."

"Well, I like those big peppermints, the ones that look like little pillows and melt in your mouth. Bring me some of those next time you come."

"Okay, I will."

"Now go on."

"What?" Letty shook her head, wondering if she had heard right.

"You heard me. Go on. I've had enough of you."

"But, Aunt Letty, I just got here."

"What do you expect me to do? Dance a jig of happiness because someone deigned to visit? You go on, and when you come back, bring me those peppermints."

"Okay." Letty was reluctant to leave. She took one more look at the birds, trying to come up with something to salvage the afternoon. When she looked at her aunt, she was staring at her.

"You still here? I thought I told you to go."

"You did. I'm sorry. I'll go."

"As long as you're here, make yourself useful."

"How?"

"Get me some water, or some lemonade. Nice and cold. Can you do that?"

"I'll see if I can." Letty approached one of the uniformed staff. "My aunt would like some water or lemonade. Is there somewhere I can get her some?"

"Yes. I'll show you to the dining area. We have drinks available for our residents all day."

"Thank you." Letty came back with some lemonade in a paper cup with a lid on it and a straw.

"Who are you?" her aunt asked.

"I'm your niece, Letty. Don't you remember?"

"Of course I remember my niece, my namesake, but you're not her."

"What do you mean, Auntie. I am her."

"No, she's much younger than you are. She's a dancer. She's in New York, dancing with Alvin Ailey. She sent me this card." Aunt Letty pulled out a card from a bag in her wheelchair.

Letty looked at the postcard from New York. She hadn't sent it. It must have been from her mother when she was there visiting.

"No, Aunt Letty. It's me. I'm home from New York. I'm in Detroit now."

"You aren't my niece. Don't you be trying to fool me none. You get out of here or I'll call the police."

"But Aunt Letty …" Letty took her hands and tried to get her to look in her eyes.

"Don't you touch me. Police, police, help!" her aunt cried out. Letty let go of her aunt's hands, backed off and looked around the room as her aunt continued to call for help. Nursing staff came in, walked past her to her aunt.

"It's all right, Mrs. Burke. What do you want?"

"That girl. She claims she's my niece. She just wants my money." Vicky Taylor came into the room as well.

"She is your niece, Mrs. Burke," Vicky said.

"No, she's not. My niece is in New York."

Vicky looked over at Letty as staff tried to calm down her aunt. "I'm sorry. I think it would be better if you left. I'll walk you out."

"Is she always like this?" Letty asked.

"Oh, she has better days, days when she is more lucid."

"Is there anything I can do?" Letty regretted the question even as she asked it.

"If you came back to visit, it might help. After a while she will get used to you. Residents who have visitors usually do better cognitively and emotionally. Can you come back?"

"I don't know. I'm pretty busy," Letty explained.

"That's okay. I understand if you don't want to. It's hard to make the trip here then have your loved one not recognize you."

"No, that's not it," Letty tried to explain, but she couldn't come up with an appropriate lie to get her off the hook.

"Then what is it?" Vicky waited for Letty.

Letty paused, shook her head then said, "Nothing. It's nothing. I'll be back."

"That would be wonderful," Vicky said as Letty signed out.

What had her mom gotten her into, Letty wondered as she drove away? She didn't have time to visit someone who didn't even know her. It was hard enough to find time for the people who knew her, what with trying to get the Dance Studio open. Why did she have to visit her? It's not like she was her mother. She was just her great aunt.

But if she didn't, who would?

Chapter 10

As September approached and the building still wasn't ready, Letty began to wonder whether it ever would become a reality.

"Don't worry, Letty. These things always happen when you are dealing with old buildings. I didn't think we would ever get our house up to code when we first bought it, but now it's been over seven years," Sara assured her.

"I don't have seven years to wait."

"It will happen. All in God's time."

"Well, I'd like it if God's time were more on my time. You know I'm using my savings while I'm waiting to get this place up and running. Even with staying in your apartment for free, I can't do this forever." The board's agreement with Letty was that she would be able to keep what she made at the Dance Studio. They would provide the building, she would operate rent free for the first two years. After that, they would negotiate rent for the space. The board was not in a position to pay salaries. They barely had enough money to buy the building, pay taxes and fix it up. Letty had known that when she signed on. She was familiar with how hard it was to get a non-profit off the ground. Unless you had some wealthy donor, you were dependent on volunteers until you built up a donor base. She was also familiar with what it took to get a dance studio going. That had been part of her training with Alvin Ailey II. It had been training in dance, but she also learned about the business side of running a dance studio.

She had been ready to leave New York, ready for a new challenge. But now that she was living here, watching her savings be chipped away, with no other source of income, she found herself lying awake at night, doing numbers in her head. She figured she had enough for six months, maybe even one year if she was careful and continued to live rent free at Sara's, but she didn't want to wait that long to see a return on her dreams.

When September arrived and the building still wasn't ready, Letty went into panic mode.

"Sara, what am I going to do? I have to have some income. Even if the building was ready next week, it's too late to register students. The earliest we can start will be October."

"That will work, Letty. Kids are so busy when school starts. Their parents will appreciate having the break."

"Or they will already have their schedule filled up before we even open. It's not like we already have an established group of students. We're starting from scratch here."

"I've got an idea. What if, instead of waiting for the building to be ready for classes, you took your classes to the students?" Sara suggested.

"What are you talking about?"

"My twins are in a progressive, culturally mixed school. What if you offered classes at the school, after school was out? You could do some of those different cultural dances you keep talking about."

"Do you think the school would let me? Wouldn't I be competing with their own after-school programs? And would the parents be willing to pay for such classes?"

"It won't cost any more than putting them in latch key, and look what they would get for it. Dance lessons from an Alvin Ailey dancer. Trust me. I know the other parents. They will love the idea."

Sara got a group of parents together, convinced them about the idea, then approached the principal.

"Just think how good it will look in your advertisements for your school. Multi-cultural dance classes," Sara pitched the idea as Letty stood by her side.

Letty's shoulders relaxed when the principal agreed to classes twice a week. She hadn't realized how tense she had been.

"It's not a lot, but it's a start," Sara said afterwards.

"It's more than a start. It's an answer to my prayers." Letty hugged her. "Maybe I could get into other schools. Maybe offer classes during the day too, as part of the curriculum."

"Slow down. Don't spread yourself too thin," Sara warned. "You still have to get the dance studio off the ground. We need to set up some classes and start advertising them."

They agreed upon a start date of the first week of October to begin offering classes at Freedom House.

"You're sure the building will be ready by then?" Letty asked at the September board meeting.

"We may not be ready for the grand opening we want to have to launch the building, but we should be ready to offer classes. Now that we've got all the permits, the only hold up will be getting the city inspector into the building to approve our work," Derrick said.

"Wait, I thought you've been working on that for months," Letty said.

"I have, but this city is a large bureaucracy. It moves slow."

"Do we have any recourse if we are ready to start classes and we can't get the building inspector's approval?" Letty asked.

"I've got some connections," Derrick said. "We do have some legal recourse. Hopefully we won't have to use them. If we do, I have some favors I can call in."

Letty was reassured by that and began passing out brochures and posting fliers throughout the city. She was starting out small, offering classes after school and evenings on those days she wasn't tied up at Sara's kids' school. She was focusing on beginner classes, beginner ballet, and pre-school dance, though she was hoping to get enough students for lyrical dance and modern dance. Once she had a clientele developed, she would have a better idea where the interest lay and add classes based on that. She also would offer some weekend workshops. She had the space, now she just needed the students.

Letty came back to visit her aunt Letty, each time bringing the peppermints she had requested. Some days her aunt knew her. Others she didn't. Over time she was establishing a rapport with her aunt. She was able to get bits of history out of her on her more lucid days.

"Your many times great grandfather, he was the first black barber that Cascade Falls had. He learned the trade as a slave on a plantation. His wife was a seamstress. I don't know whether she learned that while a slave or after being free. I do know they were among the first black middle class in Cascade Falls. They helped start the First Baptist Church."

"Then how did my family become African Methodist Episcopal, AME?"

"Oh, they were too uppity to go to a black Baptist church with all that gospel music and being slain in the spirit."

"Really? When did that happen?"

"That was your grandma's doings, my sister. She liked the quieter, more dignified service of the AME, or so she told me. I told her she needed to remember her roots. She didn't pay me no mind. Never did. You got any more of those peppermints?"

"Just the ones I gave you."

"You bring me more the next time you visit."

"I will, Auntie." Other times her aunt didn't recognize her and threw her out. Or she thought Letty was her daughter Ella, or her sister's daughter, Alicia, Letty's mother. Letty kept coming back. The staff all knew her and warned her ahead of time what to expect. They also told her how much her aunt looked forward to her visits.

"She's always bragging on you as the Alvin Ailey dancer," they told her.

At least someone believed in her.

Letty sighed as she looked over her list of students. She hadn't filled any of the classes. Her best response was to the pre-K classes and beginning ballet classes. She had kept the price low to be in line with her competition. Her status as a former dancer with Alvin Ailey didn't go far here, unlike Cascade Falls.

"That's because they don't know you yet. You're a newcomer. Give it some time. Eventually everyone else will start to realize how amazing you are," Sara told her.

Letty didn't feel amazing as she worked with the handful of students she had. At this rate, she would hardly have enough students for a recital.

"So you start out small. Have a small recital for the students you have. Eventually word will get out," Sara assured her. The classes at Sara's school were going well. They were non-traditional. Everyone with any skill level participated. It was fun for the kids, and for Letty.

"Maybe we should just focus on these classes," Letty suggested.

"No, the idea is to use the building."

"But if people don't want to drive into downtown Detroit for dance classes …"

"Then, maybe we need to work on the other aspects of the building," Sara suggested.

"Such as?" Letty didn't like where this was going.

"Researching the history of the Underground Railroad in Detroit, setting up a museum, setting up studio space for struggling artists and displaying their work. That was all part of the plan."

"That's not exactly what I signed up for."

"Yes, but you can do it. You do the research. I'll work on the studio and art gallery. Eventually we might even be able to pay you for this, once we get it off the ground."

Letty was skeptical, but intrigued as well. What else did she have to do with her time during the day?

Chapter 11

Cascade Falls – Present Day

Joe was used to meeting with the high school principal. As pastor, he was kept abreast of what was happening at the church school—activities, problems with students, staff. He served as a default principal at times when the principal needed back up. Still he hadn't been expecting a visit from Mrs. Allen before their regular Friday meeting. He welcomed her and sat back down at his desk. She pulled up a chair across from him.

"Pastor, I know you are busy, so I'll get right to the point." She leaned forward in the chair. Conversations that started like this never went well.

"It's your niece," she said.

"My niece?"

"Yes, Ashley Reese." Oh yes. Joe hadn't quite gotten used to the fact that with his marriage, he had inherited two nieces and a nephew. What had Ashley done now? He had known this day would come. Didn't make it any easier now that it had. Could it be any worse than what he had gone through with his daughter, Stephanie?

"What happened?"

"She's causing problems in her religion class."

"What kinds of problems?" He hated to guess. God only knows what might be going on in the mind of that child.

"She says she doesn't believe in God."

"Oh," Joe leaned back and sighed. "Are you sure she didn't say she was just questioning whether God existed? That's a normal question for teenagers to struggle with."

"No, she says there is no God. You can imagine the problems it's creating." He could imagine. Joe wondered who Ashley was really upsetting.

"I'll talk to her."

"You better, and you better set her straight or she may need to find another school to attend," Mrs. Allen said as she stood up.

"I'll take care of it. Thank you for bringing it to my attention."

What to do, Joe wondered after she left. Ashley had always been a precocious child, one who didn't accept easy answers, who liked to challenge everything. He had expected there would be trouble eventually, but he had expected something more along the lines of what Stephanie had done, acting out, rebelling, partying. However, Ashley was not the party type. Since last spring she had been so committed to her dancing, he thought she would be able to make it through high school without any problems. Ashley was too committed to dance and the discipline of ballet to go out partying. This, he hadn't expected, though now that it had happened it seemed so obvious. Ashley was her own person. She had always struck him as someone who would chart her own course in life, challenging pre-conceived ideas. How to approach this?

He would have to let her father know. What would Dale say? And Kathleen, her aunt, his wife? What would she say? He had to handle the situation with care. Several years ago, Joe had seen Ashley for counseling. The relationship was amicable, if not close. He knew Kathleen had felt hurt when Ashley no longer wanted to keep their monthly diner dates and sleepovers once she married. Kathleen worried about Ashley, as did he. But Ashley was strong. There was an inner core of strength in that girl.

First, he would talk to Dale. That would be the easy part. Then he would worry about Kathleen.

Chapter 12

Cascade Falls – Present Day

Another set-up. Letty couldn't believe her mother was still trying to fix her up with local men, usually lawyers or other professionals. The fact that she always managed to dodge out as soon as possible during each set-up didn't deter her mother.

She had come home to have her foot checked. This time, she hoped she would be given the okay to start dancing again. Her hope had been fulfilled. Now all she had to do was get through the obligatory meal then she would escape to her uncle's club and dance the night away.

She could tell her "date," Walter, didn't want to be there for dinner any more than she did. His parents had set it up for him. They were new members of her parents' church, recently moved to town, and they had a single son who also happened to be a lawyer. What more could her mother have asked for? Except, of course, her mother never asked her.

Walter made excuses to leave even before her, faking an emergency phone call. Letty knew about this since she employed the same strategy to get out of dates that weren't going well. But he left her, not just with her parents, but with his parents. Who would do that? Letty just wished she had thought of a way out of the dinner sooner.

"Leticia, your parents tell me you are a dancer," Walter's mother, Mrs. Treadwell, said.

"That's right."

"My baby is a dancer with Alvin Ailey," her mother jumped in.

"My, impressive," Mrs. Treadwell said.

"Was, Mom — was," Letty corrected.

"What are you doing now?" Mrs. Treadwell asked.

"I'm starting an alternative dance school in Detroit."

"How alternative?" Mr. Treadwell spoke up.

"I'll be using some of what I learned through Alvin Ailey. There'll be some traditional classes, but what I really want to do is open up dance to all age groups, all income levels, all skill levels. I plan to have intergenerational classes and mash-ups of different dance styles, including traditional cultural dances and hip-hop."

"Hip-hop?" Mrs. Treadwell said.

"Yes, it is the cultural dance of the day."

"My Walter is a dreamer too," Mrs. Treadwell said.

"Is that so?" Letty looked at her phone, pretending to answer a text. "Look at the time. I've got to go."

"So soon. We haven't had dessert yet," her mother said.

"You know I don't eat dessert," Letty reminded her. "You four enjoy. It was nice meeting you." The lie slid out easily on her tongue from years of practice in regards to her mother's dinner dates. She let out a sigh of relief as she slipped out the door. Time to get to her uncle Delbert's club.

She had been working her foot gradually all this time, stretching, regaining strength. Her doctor had been pleased with her progress. He had even given her the okay to dance, within reason. She couldn't wait to test her recovery. She was meeting Chloe and her boyfriend there. She hoped her friend and favorite dancing partner Omar was there.

"How was the set-up?" Chloe asked when she arrived.

Letty just raised her eyebrows and shook her head.

"That bad?"

"He didn't even stay till the end of the meal. What was worse, he left me there with his parents."

"That bad. Let's get you a drink." Chloe waited while Letty gave the waitress her order.

Letty sipped her white wine, all she allowed herself because of calories. "Enough of that. I came here to dance." She looked about the room for a likely dance partner, then pulled back in surprise when she saw Walter.

"That guy. Collared shirt, dress slacks," Letty pointed him out to Chloe. "That was my set-up."

"Hmmm," Chloe found him amidst the sea of dark faces. Hers was one of the few white faces in the club. "Not bad. I wouldn't mind being set up with him."

"Hey," her boyfriend Chris said. "Remember me?"

"Of course, I do. I'm just looking out for my friend here." Chloe smiled over at Walter.

"Don't," Letty said. "I don't want him to see me."

"Too late. He's coming."

"I don't believe I know you," Walter said as he approached Chloe.

"No, but you do know my friend here." Chloe stepped aside and pulled Letty forward.

"So, this is your emergency," Letty said. Chloe slipped off to the dance floor with Chris. Letty glared at her before turning back to Walter.

"Hey, it wasn't you. Dinner with my parents and their friends? Really? Not my idea of a fun night, no matter how delightful their daughter is."

"You left me with your parents."

"Let me make it up to you. I'll buy you a drink."

"No, thank you. I've already had one. My limit. Dancers have to watch their weight."

"But I understand you aren't dancing with Alvin Ailey anymore."

"Who told you?"

"My mother told me about Alvin Ailey. Then I did a little checking on my own."

"You did?"

"Hey, a set-up by my parents? I wouldn't have even come except I found your dancing so intriguing." Walter grinned at her as if confident his engaging smile would win her over. Letty wasn't about to be won over so easily.

"Then why did you leave?" Letty gazed about the club, feigning indifference.

"It actually was business related. I had to meet a client here."

"And where is that client now?"

"My, are you sure you aren't a lawyer? All these questions. Will I get a chance to cross examine?"

"Answer the question, counsellor." She turned to confront him.

"Business done. I thought I'd enjoy myself."

"And are you? Enjoying yourself that is?"

"That's yet to be determined." He raised his eyebrows, clinked her glass with his beer and smiled.

"Letty, we've got to dance," Omar appeared from out of the crowd, grabbed her arm and pulled her out on the dance floor. Letty glanced back at Walter who was still looking at her. He raised his beer in salute then finished it off. Letty turned back to the dance floor, laughed and gave herself over to the music, testing her limits.

After two dances, Letty threw herself down on a chair at an open table as she regained her breath. She was rusty but her foot wasn't complaining too much. Her partner pulled up a chair next to her.

"I'm sorry if I rescued you when you didn't want to be rescued."

Letty scanned the room for Walter. Nowhere in sight.

"Who was that gorgeous hunk of man, anyway?" Omar asked.

"The son of a friend of my parents."

"Oh, a set-up. Well, if you're not interested …?"

Letty laughed and got back up, pulling Omar with her. "I came here to dance, not talk," she said and went back out on the dance floor. One more dance, then she would head home.

Chapter 13

Cascade County – 1853

Nathaniel pulled a trunk off of the stage coach and carried it into the hotel lobby. He waited while the owner, a white man of some seeming importance, signed in, his equally important wife fussing with her gloves and surveying the hotel lobby with an air of disdain.

"Boy," the man motioned to Nathaniel to follow him. He carried the trunk up two flights of stairs and placed it in the hotel room. For his services he received a penny.

Such was his day. Hauling luggage to and from rooms in the Empire Hotel, one of two such establishments in the bustling city of Cascade Falls. The nearby train station was a hub of activity bringing weary travelers to this popular stop along the route between Detroit and Chicago. Nathaniel's wages were kept for him by the couple who ran the poorhouse where he resided with others unable to find a place to live that they could afford. He was saving to be able to someday start his own barbershop. But for now, he was content with his lot in life, working the farm that provided vegetables for the poorhouse and working at the hotel for tips. He managed to remain hidden while in plain sight.

During the six years that he had lived there, he had developed friendships and gained the trust of the abolitionists in town. He attended the one church in town that welcomed colored people. Still he remained wary, especially since the Fugitive Slave Act had passed three years ago. The act required local officials to cooperate in the return of runaway slaves. Six years was a long time, but his master had a long memory. He had been known to go longer and farther to catch a horse thief. His master remembered every injustice, real or imagined, that he had received over the years, keeping track in an internal ledger book in his head. Nathaniel knew this from what he had heard at times while shaving him.

Nathaniel had not wanted to be counted in the 1850 national census but had been caught unaware when the census taker showed up at the poorhouse. Too late to run away, he had given his name but not his correct birthplace. For months after that he had feared hearing a knock on the door and seeing the face of his master coming to claim what was rightfully his. He was no man's property, he knew, but the courts were against him. A piece of paper was all it took to take away his freedom. When years passed and there was no knock, he hoped maybe he had been able to once again pass unnoticed.

Josiah Whitcomb had made arrangements for him to stay at the poorhouse and had since served as a sponsor for him, helping him out with the requirements to remain safe while building a new life. He trusted him as much as he trusted any white man, more as the years progressed. Nathaniel knew how to dissemble, give the white folk what they wanted. He had learned well during those years on the plantation. The masters, they paid no attention to the slaves as long as they did what they were told. But the slaves, they watched and learned because their lives depended on it. They knew the tell-tale signs that the overseer was having a bad day because that bad day would be acted out upon them. They knew when the master was looking lonely and wanting company. Only they weren't able to hide their wives and daughters. To interfere against the master's demands would warrant a whipping. It was supposed to be a privilege when the master chose a woman to share his bed. And then they were to raise any children born of such a union as their own.

No, Nathaniel knew the ways of the white men on the plantation. He knew sometimes they behaved as if they were friends, but they could not be trusted. They could turn against you just as easily and you had no recourse. Nathaniel knew this, but some of the white folk up here, some that he had gotten to know … he could almost trust them, had to trust them, for if not they could have handed him over at any time. It was a precarious position to live in, but better than the life he had known as a slave. Nathaniel continued to have dreams of having his own barber shop but was afraid it would draw too much attention. He kept his scissors sharp and hidden away. His master would be looking for a barber, but not for a porter living in a poorhouse. He didn't dare give up his cover, even now after six years.

Nathaniel was not surprised when Josiah Whitcomb showed up at the hotel. He often met clients there or ate lunch in the dining room. Josiah always had a kind word for Nathaniel. But today there was something wrong. Nathaniel knew it the minute he saw him.

"Nathaniel, come with me," he instructed.

Nathaniel left immediately, not even taking time to let anyone know he was leaving.

Josiah led him to his office, closed the door and explained. "There is someone here looking for you. Says he is your owner and has papers to reclaim his property."

"What we goin' to do?" Nathaniel's eyes remained expressionless, his voice calm. He had long learned to hide his emotions from white folk.

"We are moving you, tonight. As soon as it is dark. We will be taking you to Detroit where you can pass to Canada." Nathaniel nodded his head in agreement. No discussion needed. "I will get your things from the poorhouse and make sure you have money for the journey," Josiah assured him before he even asked.

"Thank you kindly, sir," Nathaniel said, placing his life, once again, in the hands of a white man. Josiah looked directly into his eyes and placed his hand on Nathaniel's shoulder

"We can't wait. You understand that?" Nathaniel nodded his head, yes. "We will get you safely on your way. I promise."

Nathaniel looked back into the man's eyes. He believed him.

Chapter 14

Detroit – Present Day

The board approved the plans to go forward with setting up a museum featuring the history of the house and its role in the Underground Railroad. As part of her research, Letty was meeting Derrick for lunch at a downtown deli.

"Seems funny, me being the one with the notebook and pen," Letty said as she pulled out her notebook and prepared to write. Her attempt at humor was met with a stare.

"I don't have a lot of time. Let's get started."

"Okay. Aren't you eating?" Letty asked when he waved off the waitress after she ordered a bowl of soup.

"I'll take a sandwich back to my office. I don't like to mix meals with business. Gets too messy."

"So, this is business?"

"What else would it be? It's about Freedom House."

"Right, but I thought … never mind. Let's get down to business."

"Before you ask, I've already written down significant dates in regards to the house." He passed her several sheets of paper from a folder.

"That's good. This will be helpful."

"As you can see, the house was built in the 1830's. It was meant to be a show place."

"A show place? For what?"

"My great grandparent's wealth. What else? Or more accurately, my great grandfather's wealth. My great grandmother wasn't as interested in wealth or showing off. Here's her picture." Derrick handed her the manila folder with pictures and pointed out a black and white photo of a woman in a bonnet.

"I don't know how they ever got together, my great grandfather and great grandmother. They were so different. But I guess marriage was different back then. Not all of this mumbo jumbo about love and whatnot."

"Are you saying theirs was a marriage of convenience?"

"I think my great grandfather married my great grandmother for her status in the community. She was from one of the leading families at that time. Doesn't mean they didn't come to love each other, in their own way."

"So, they built the house in the 1830's. How old were they then?"

"If you look at the sheet I prepared, you'll see their birthdates. If I have to keep going over what is there in front of you, we will never get done."

"Okay, I see it." Letty fought the surge of anger at his comment. If she got angry at every one of his rude comments, she would never get the information she needed. Besides, she had promised Sara she would play nice. "Your great grandfather Owen Jacobson was born in 1791. That would make him in his forties. Your great grandmother, Priscilla, was born in 1800, so she'd have been in her thirties."

"That's right."

"Were they both abolitionists?"

"No, my great grandfather Owen was a business man. As such he didn't concern himself about other people's properties."

"Properties? Are you saying slaves were just properties?" Letty knew what she had promised Sara, but really …

"I'm just saying what my great grandfather would have said."

Letty bit her tongue. Just get through lunch, get the information she needed. "Did he have slaves himself?"

"No, he grew up poor, the son of German immigrants. He worked hard, trading goods, until he became the owner of the largest mercantile in Detroit."

"And your great grandmother Priscilla?"

"She was the abolitionist. Always had strong ideas. At least, that's what my grandmother told me about her. I've got a journal written by her. Doesn't recount much, but I believe it's a record of abolitionist activity."

"Did you bring it with you?" Now she was getting somewhere.

"Yes." Derrick pulled out an old ledger. He carefully opened it and showed Letty a page written in a neat, feminine script. "See, she notes down cargo, arrival date and departure date. I believe this was her record of the runaway slaves that passed through her home. It starts in the 1840s, ends in the 1860s after the Civil War."

"How do you know this wasn't your great grandfather Owen's business ledger?"

"I've got other ledgers of my great grandfather's. The writing is different and the notations are more detailed."

Letty looked over the entries, intrigued despite her resistance to Derrick's manners. "Saturday, Oct. 21, 2 parcels delivered, shipped out Sunday, Oct. 22." That was unusual, she thought. She closed her eyes to think. "They wouldn't have been open for business on Sunday back then," she commented. "But they would do the Lord's work on Sunday."

"Precisely."

Letty looked at other entries. Sometimes as many as six parcels. More often one or two. "Can I keep this?"

"I'd rather keep it myself. I plan to donate them to the museum, but I want to make sure they are properly preserved."

"And the pictures?"

"Same thing." Derrick pulled the folder away from her as the waitress brought her soup. "You understand now why I didn't want to take my chances with food around them."

"Yes, I understand." Letty regretted her order. She carefully spooned the hot liquid into her mouth as she looked over the typed sheets Derrick had given her.

"Would you let me have a look at that ledger another time? Maybe at the house?"

"That could be arranged."

"Or, I would love to have copies of the ledger. Do you think you could make copies for me?"

"Might be hard to make copies without breaking the binding." Derrick put the folder back in his briefcase and prepared to leave.

"I understand. It's just, I'd like to have a record of how many slaves total passed through that house."

"I can get you that."

"And we'll want to put the original ledger in a glass case for people to see, along with the pictures."

"Yes. I would like that. That house, it holds many memories from visiting my grandparents as a child. My grandmother told me many stories about those early years, ones that had been passed on to her from her grandparents. I want to see that history preserved."

"I understand." Was he softening? "Do you think you could meet me at the house some day? Walk me through the building, this time without your clipboard. I'd like to hear your stories."

"That could be arranged," Derrick agreed.

Letty planned to walk back from the deli to Freedom House. A chilly breeze from the Detroit River cut into her as she walked along the sidewalk. She stopped to look at the statue of a runaway slave looking across the river to freedom on the other shore. What had he been thinking as he looked across that body of water? Did it seem too deep, too far, impassable? Or was it just another obstacle on his journey to freedom? How many obstacles had he conquered on his way? How many rivers to cross, hills to climb, dogs to outrun?

A number of the dances she had done at Alvin Ailey were focused on freedom. She hadn't thought that much about them at the time. Now, as she learned more about her own history, the history of this city and the building that had become part of her life, those dances took on more meaning in her memory. If only she had realized this when she had been dancing them.

Letty shivered as the breeze kicked up from the river. She decided against the long walk and hailed a cab. Once there she peered through the pages Derrick had given her and started to look about the building with fresh eyes. She hoped in their rush to clean the place they hadn't thrown out anything of importance. She went down to the storage room in the basement and started to pull out boxes that had been placed there. What she was looking for, she wasn't sure. She figured she would know when she saw it. She remained there, engrossed in her work until a glance at her watch reminded her she needed to get ready for her first class.

Tomorrow would be time enough to continue her search.

Chapter 15

Joe called Dale over the weekend and let him know about what was going on with Ashley.

"I didn't know, but I'm not surprised. Ashley goes to church with us, reluctantly, then slouches in the pew and doesn't participate. She doesn't even go to youth group any more. She hasn't said why, just that she didn't want to go. Do you want me to talk to her?"

"If you don't mind, I'd rather talk to her first. You have to be careful not to push her into a position where she feels forced to take a stand and not budge." Dale had agreed to let him try. He decided not to tell Kathleen, not till he talked to Ashley.

He arranged for Ashley to come over to the parish office to see him during her religion class. He knew Ashley would be happy for any excuse to get out of religion. Ashley plopped down in her accustomed seat from their previous counseling sessions and waited for him to start the conversation.

"Ashley, good to see you."

"Is it? Isn't being called to the pastor's office much like being sent to the vice principal's office?"

"You don't seem too upset about it."

"Any time I get out of religion class is good for me. We could make this a regular routine."

"Do you know why you are here?"

"No, but I can guess. Does it have anything to do with me being an atheist?"

"Right to the point." This girl didn't waste any time.

"So, what are you going to do about it?"

"What can I do if you've already made up your mind?"

"You aren't going to try and talk me out of it?" Joe could hear the surprise in Ashley's voice, almost disappointment. Had she expected more of a rise out of him? She wasn't going to get it.

"Is that possible?"

"No, but I thought you would try."

"That's not what I'm here for. But I would like to know more about your decision."

"What's to know, Pastor? I'm not a kid any more. I don't believe in fairy tales, Santa Claus or the Easter bunny. Why should I believe in God?"

"You put God in the same category as Santa Claus and the Easter Bunny?" Clearly, this was not going to be easy. Joe rested his chin on his hand as he stared into her face.

"It's just what you tell people so they don't feel so bad about their lives. I don't need a crutch. Opiate of the masses, Karl Marx says."

"So, you've done your research?"

"Yes, I have. I didn't just decide overnight. I've been thinking about it, reading about it."

"Really? What have you been reading?" Joe raised an eyebrow and leaned back in his chair.

"Famous atheists, philosophers, Stephen Hawking."

"Did you try reading any famous atheists who converted, like C.S. Lewis? He was an atheist during his youth, then became one of the most famous theologians of the twentieth century."

"I know his Narnia stories for kids, but I'm not a kid anymore. I don't believe in Narnia any more than I believe in heaven."

"You don't believe in heaven?" Joe asked.

"No, there's just this earth, this life, in this space in time. After we die, our bodies go back into the earth as food for new life."

"What if I give you other writings by Lewis, not kid stories? Would you read them?"

"I guess, if I have time. I'm pretty busy with dance."

"I know, your Aunt Kathleen says you've become her most dedicated dancer."

Ashley shrugged her shoulders at this.

"Your mom would be proud of you," he added.

"You think so. I'm not doing this for her, you know." Ashley squirmed at the mention of her mom. Perhaps he had found a way in.

"Then who are you doing this for?"

"For me. I like dancing and it seems I'm good at it."

"You are. But about your mom … if there is no heaven, what about your mom?"

"If you are going to give me that your-mom-is-watching-from-heaven stuff, forget it. I don't believe that. Even if there is a heaven, I doubt mom would be wasting her time with the goings on here on earth."

"What would she be doing?" Joe leaned forward in an attempt to engage Ashley further.

"I think she would be dancing. She would be part of the heavenly chorus. But that's if I believed in heaven, which I don't." Ashley leaned back in response to Joe's attempt to engage her.

"So, where does that put your mom?"

"She's in me, in my genetic make-up, in my memory. That's all."

"Nothing more?"

"No, nothing more."

Joe leaned back in his chair, clasped his hands together and rested his chin on them as he processed what she had said. "You seem to have given this a lot of thought."

"I'm not a baby, Pastor. I can think for myself, make my own decisions."

"That you can. You aren't a baby. As you grow older, it's important that you make a free choice to believe in God, instead of just accepting what your parents tell you."

"Or not. A free choice to not believe."

"Yes, if that weren't an option, then it wouldn't be a free choice." Joe lowered his hands onto his desk.

"And I've made my choice."

"That you have." Joe could see that. There was no changing her mind, at least not today. "And you can change that choice any time you want."

"Are we done?" Ashley shifted forward as if preparing to leave. "Not that I'm in a hurry to get back to religion class."

"About that, could you do me a favor?"

"That depends on the favor."

"Could you not say anything in religion class about being an atheist?"

"Do you want me to lie?"

"No, not lie. Just keep your opinions to yourself. Seems it's upsetting people."

"You mean it's upsetting my teacher. She can't handle it whenever I say I'm an atheist."

"And other people too."

"She's afraid I'm going to lead other people to my way of thinking."

"Maybe."

"Does this mean I can get out of religion class?" Ashley cocked her head and smiled slightly.

"No, that's not for me to decide. You know the school policy. All students take religion classes every year. I can't interfere with that."

"You are the Pastor."

Ashley certainly was a challenge.

"That only goes so far. I doubt your principal wants to set a precedent and have other students try to get out of religion class."

"Then I guess if I have to keep attending, I'll keep telling everyone what I think." Ashley shrugged her shoulders and leaned back in her chair.

"Look, Ashley. You're a junior. The year's partially over. That means you only have a year and a half left to take religion classes. That's not too long."

"Why can't I get out early so I can warm up for dance class? Get early release?"

"I'll see what I can do, but no promises." Joe sat back with a sigh and made a note.

"Does this mean I don't have to go to church anymore?"

"That's between you and your parents."

"But you will tell my dad about our talk?" Ashley persisted.

"Your father already knows we are meeting and why. But you know what we say here is confidential. All I can tell him is that we met, unless you give me permission to discuss it with him."

"Sure. You can talk to him. Tell him what you want."

"I'd rather you tell him."

"Okay. Can I go now?" Ashley stood up and tossed her long pony tail.

"One more thing." Joe stopped her. "Your Aunt Kathleen doesn't know we are meeting. Is it all right if I tell her?"

"Tell her anything you want. It's no secret."

"You know, Ashley," Joe stood up to walk her to the door. "Just because you don't believe in God, doesn't mean God doesn't believe in you. God will be there for you, anytime you want."

"Sure. Whatever," Ashley said. With that Ashley left, leaving Joe shaking his head.

Chapter 16

Detroit – Present Day

"You've been working too hard," Sara told her. "And spending too much time with us old married folks."

"Hey, speak for yourself," said Larry, Sara's husband. "Thirty isn't that old."

Nights that Letty wasn't at the dance studio, Sara would invite her to have dinner with her family.

"I'm speaking for myself. I'm thinking you need some time out. Time out with single people your own age. I'm going to take you clubbing."

"You aren't exactly single," Larry stated.

"I know, but someone has to show Letty around and someone has to stay here and babysit. Guess who that someone is?"

"I guess that would be me," Larry said. "Don't you have any friends from when you took those dance classes here?"

"That's been seven years," Letty said. "The only people I know now are you and Sara and the other members of the board of directors."

"We definitely have to do something about that," Sara said.

Sara invited Chloe to stay overnight so they could have a girl's night out.

"I haven't been out since the last time we went to my Uncle Delbert's," Letty said as they got into a cab.

"That's way too long, girl," Chloe said. "Sara, you got her locked up or something?"

"I just needed you here to get her to agree to go out. There's a number of clubs within walking distance," Sara told them when they arrived. "We can hit them all."

"You lead the way," Letty said. Her one drink rule was going to be suspended this night.

The first place was rather tame. They nursed one drink then decided to move on. A few couples were on the dance floor but not enough to entice them to join them.

"Maybe it heats up later," Sara said. "Maybe we came out too early. Some places are just getting started at eleven."

"Eleven? That's my bed time," Chloe said.

"Not tonight. We'll keep going till we find some fun," Sara said.

"Or make our own fun," Letty added.

"Now I like that," Sara agreed. They finished off their drinks and headed outside to find another club. Down the street they saw groups of people outside a door.

"Let's try that one," Letty suggested.

When they arrived, there was a line. Most of the people in the line were younger than them. "We can fit in with this crowd," Letty insisted.

"You think? I didn't come out to feel old. I'm the oldest one in line," Sara said.

"Just don't act old. Come on." Letty started for the end of the line.

"Letty?" she heard a voice call her name.

"Walter?" she said when she turned around. "What are you doing here?"

"I could ask you the same."

"I live here, in Detroit. You know that."

"That's right. I live here too."

"You didn't tell me that."

"One of the few questions you didn't ask me that night." Walter smiled.

"Letty," Sara interrupted their conversation. "Are you going to introduce us?"

"I think we've already met, at Delbert's. I'm Chloe." Chloe stepped forward and extended her hand.

"Yes, Letty's enchanting friend," he took her hand into his and smiled.

"Wooh," Chloe swooned in response. "He's a charmer. If not for Chris …," Chloe stated as she pretended to fan her face.

"Do you want to join me and my friends?" Walter pointed to the front of the line where two of his friends were waving at him.

Letty looked at Chloe and Sara, then said yes for all of them. "Sure. Why not?"

They pushed their way through the crowded night club, following close behind Walter. Some other friends of Walter's had saved them a table.

"We need three more chairs," Walter said above the uproar. His friends jumped up, grabbed chairs from other tables and crowded them around their table as Walter introduced them. Letty struggled to hear through all the noise.

"Now, about that drink I owe you. White wine?" Letty nodded yes. He ordered drinks for all three of them. "That was some dancing the other night at your uncle's." Walter leaned in close to make sure she heard.

"You noticed?"

"How could I not? How could anyone not notice the two of you? You dominated the dance floor with your partner. Boyfriend?"

"Just a dance partner. We have fun dancing together."

"I could see that."

"Why didn't you stick around?"

"The girl I was interested in wasn't interested in me."

"How did you know that?" Letty took a sip of wine, gazing at him over the rim of the glass.

"She was dancing with some other guy. Besides, I needed to get back to Detroit that night. Had business the next morning."

"Sunday morning?"

"No rest for the wicked."

"Well, you better not let that happen again." She put her wine glass down.

"What's that?"

"Let some other guy dance with your girl." Letty smiled and nodded at the dance floor. "You game?"

"I can promise that I'm not as good as your other dance partner."

"That's okay. I'll lead."

The night whirled by. Walter, while not Omar, proved to be a not-too-shabby dancer. Sara and Chloe spent the night getting to know Walter's friends.

"Did you know they were all lawyers?" Sara said during the ride home.

"Why didn't you tell me? We could have ditched them sooner," Letty said.

"You didn't seem to be in any hurry to ditch your lawyer," Chloe added.

"He's an okay dancer," Letty smiled and shrugged her shoulders.

"Yes, we noticed. The two of you made a great couple. When are you going to see him again?" Sara asked.

"I don't know."

"You did give him your phone number," Chloe asserted.

"Yes, but will he call?" Letty shrugged her shoulders again. His business card was tucked safely away in her clutch purse.

"Oh, he'll call. And if not, I've got the phone numbers of most of his friends. They're interested in Freedom House. Maybe got some more volunteers, or board members ..." Sara waved a number of business cards in her face.

"Or donors," Letty added.

"That too," Sara grinned.

"This was supposed to be fun, not work," Letty said.

"It was fun," Chloe said as she climbed out of the Uber.

Yes, it was. More than fun, Letty admitted to herself as she glanced at Walter's business card then slipped it back into her purse.

Chapter 17

Detroit – Present Day

Chloe returned home after breakfast the next morning. Sara invited Letty to come to church with them.

"No, thanks. Maybe another time. I'm meeting Derrick at the house. He's going to walk through the building with me. Point out what he remembers about the history of each room."

"Derrick?" Sara teased. "I wouldn't have thought he was your type."

"Ha, ha. Real funny. Me and Derrick. No, this is just business."

"I'll pray for you."

Since coming to Detroit, Letty hadn't settled on any church. Sara had invited her to come to her church several times. It was a multiracial church. Sara said they had a young congregation, up-beat music, one of those mega churches.

"If you don't meet somebody there, you're hopeless. There are lots of young men and women your age. We have an active young adult ministry."

"Yes, Pastor," Letty had teased.

"I'm not a pastor"

"Then stop sounding like one trying to sell her church to me."

Mega churches just didn't strike her as right for her. Maybe she was too "uppity" as her great aunt said. She liked her home church in Cascade Falls but hadn't gone to church while she was in New York. The practice room and rehearsal hall had been her sanctuary, dance her ritual. What did she need church for?

But now, she was craving some kind of connection, the community that came with church. Maybe she was just lonely. She no longer had the dance company to act as friend and family, a buffer against the rest of the world. Maybe she could use a place of refuge like the slaves that hid in basements and cubby holes along the Underground Railroad. She wasn't sure what she was looking for.

Letty met Derrick on the front steps of the house. "Shall we?" she said as she opened the door. She thought she almost got a smile out of him. But no, that would be too much to expect.

"Where should we start?" Letty asked.

"Let's start with the basement. That's where Grandma Priscilla hid the slaves. There's a large storage area next to a smaller room, big enough to fit a cot. The slaves would stay there during the day until Grandma was able to slip them out."

"Was she hiding them from her husband?"

"Yes, he didn't know what his wife was up to. Didn't want to know. But he died in 1845, left everything to Grandma, the house and the business."

"What about his son?"

"He was a bit of a snob from what I could tell. Couldn't get his hands dirty with work. Went into law and politics instead."

"Did he know about the slaves?"

"No, Grandmother kept it a secret from him. I believe she figured as a lawyer he would have felt obligated to return the slaves under the Fugitive Slave Act of 1850."

"Did anyone in the family support your grandmother in her efforts?" Letty asked as they walked to the back of the house.

"The servants knew all about it. And her grandson. He would have kept it going had its need not ended with the Civil War."

"Your great grandmother must have been a strong woman of great character."

"The strongest. … Wait, what's that!?" Derrick said as he opened the door to the kitchen and the back stairs. "Look," he pointed to a broken window. Glass littered the floor. "It looks like someone has broken in. I know that window had been replaced." He checked the back door. "And the door is unlocked. Someone must have broken in through the window, then unlocked the door."

"What if they are still here?" Letty asked.

"We'll see."

"Shouldn't we call the police?"

"Wait." Derrick walked over to the pantry door, grabbed a broom to use as a weapon, and pulled the door open. Letty rolled her eyes at the broom but didn't stop him.

Inside was a family of four. They huddled together in a corner, their dark hair glistening against their olive brown skin in the light coming in through the door.

"Please, don't hurt us," the man said.

"What are you doing here?" Derrick asked.

"We had nowhere else to go. It was so cold. We used to stay here before. We came back because it was cold."

"Where were you staying before this?" Letty asked.

"We had been staying at the shelter, but ICE came. We can't go back there."

"What about family?" Letty continued to question him.

"It's not safe there. If ICE comes, our family will be in danger."

"Illegals," Derrick said to Letty then addressed the man. "Where are you from?"

"Honduras. We left because of the gangs. They were going to take my boy." The boy looked all of eight. "They raped my wife. I had to save my little girl." The girl looked to be six.

What was she to do? When in doubt, offer food. That much she had learned from her mother. Always offer some type of food or beverage. Whatever you had, you shared.

"Are you hungry?" Letty asked.

"Si. We have no food."

"Let's see what we have here." Letty looked through the cupboards. She had stored some food for lunches and snacks for herself. "I've got some granola bars, cheese and crackers. It's not much but you can have it." Letty coaxed them out of the pantry with the food then slipped out of the room to confer with Derrick.

"What are we going to do?" she asked.

"What can we do? They can't stay here."

"Why not? You aren't going to turn all lawyerly on me, are you?" Letty had enough with lawyers, between her brother and now Walter and his friends.

"It wouldn't be safe for them or you. We can't let every homeless person who breaks in stay."

"But the children. You aren't going to report them to ICE, are you?"

"No. We can't do that." Derrick shook his head and sat down in order to think further.

"What would your great grandmother Priscilla do?"

"That's not fair."

"Fair or not, what would she do?"

"She would have arranged passage for them to Canada."

"Would that work?" That was an interesting proposal. "Does Canada accept refugees?"

"I don't know. First, I don't know how we'd get them across the river. Second, I don't know what Canada's immigration policy is. Let me think about it."

Letty went back into the kitchen, pulled out some juice boxes she had bought for her students and gave them to the children.

"Gracias," they said, uncertain at first, then greedily gulping down the juice when their parents nodded that it was okay.

"How did you get here?" she asked their parents.

"We're migrant farmworkers. We worked the fields in Texas. We come to Michigan to work in Blissfield. When the picking was done, we moved in with family in Detroit," the man responded.

"Do you have green cards?"

"We did. They expired. When we applied for more time, they said no. Said we had to go back to Honduras. We can't go back there." The woman shook her head in agreement, letting her husband take the lead.

"Did you apply for asylum?" Derrick joined the discussion.

"We did. We were turned down. They said we were here for work, not as refugees. Said we had to go back to Honduras. They didn't believe we were in danger."

Letty looked at Derrick. "What if we got them a lawyer, someone who could help them with the legal process of getting green cards and applying for citizenship?"

"Si, senor, can you do that?" the man asked.

"I don't know. Do you know any lawyers?" Derrick asked Letty.

"In fact, I know four or five of them." Letty pulled out the business cards of Walter's friends that Sara had given her. Maybe knowing all these lawyers would serve a purpose after all.

"What do we do in the meantime?"

"We could use someone to help maintain the building, a janitor. And, the house would be more secure if someone were living here at night." Letty's brain was working.

"You mean let them live here?" Derrick asked.

"There's plenty of room."

"Don't you think that might draw suspicion?"

"What else can we do? What would Grandmother Priscilla do?" Letty knew that would get Derrick. She smiled as he squirmed, then came around to her viewpoint.

"Okay, they can stay," Derrick agreed.

"We will work," the man said.

"But we can't pay them. We can't even afford to pay you," Derrick said.

"That's okay. I'll find other work too," the Honduran said.

Derrick slowly nodded his head in agreement. "I'm going to regret this," he muttered, "but okay."

"Then it's settled," Letty said. "Let's figure out where you will sleep," she said to the family. "And can you fix that window?" she asked Derrick.

"I fix. No worry," the man said.

That wasn't what she was worried about.

Chapter 18

Detroit - 1853

Nathaniel was whirled away to safety. Driving non-stop each night, it took three nights to finally make it to Detroit as dawn broke.

"It is too late to arrange your passage to Canada this morning," the white woman at the door said as he stumbled into the large home in the midst of Detroit. His legs hardly worked after being cramped for hours in the wagon. "He will have to stay here until I can arrange passage," she told the driver — Josiah's grandson, Wesley. Wesley looked at Nathaniel.

"You will be safe here. I have to be getting home." He shook Nathaniel's hand then instructed the woman to take good care of him.

"And if you need any money for his upkeep," Wesley started to reach into his pocket. The woman stopped him, lightly placing her hand on his arm.

"You wouldn't deprive me of my right to do a kindness," she said.

"Very well then," Wesley said as he slipped out the back door.

Nathaniel looked about the spacious kitchen. There were colored people preparing breakfast. Were they slaves? Slavery had been outlawed in Michigan since the 1830s, he understood. He had been slowly learning to read, under the tutelage of Mrs. Bishop, the woman who ran the poorhouse. At night she would sit up with any of the guests who wanted to learn. She taught them by light of an oil lamp. She had also taught him about the laws that concerned slavery. His abilities were still limited but he had learned well the story of slavery in these parts.

"Nora, bring our guest some coffee," the white woman instructed.

Nathaniel sat down and accepted the mug of coffee from the colored woman.

"Nora is a servant. There are no slaves here," the white woman answered his unasked question. "She is a paid member of this household and free to come and go as she pleases, right Nora?"

"Yes, ma'am," Nora said with a smile. She came back with a large slab of bread slathered with butter and jam, then went back to her duties preparing trays for breakfast. She joked with the other servants as they worked, showing a camaraderie he remembered from his days on the plantation, but here it wasn't hidden from their mistress. There, each time the mistress had come into the kitchen, the easy laughter and chatter would come to a quick stop. Not so here. One of the servants was a white woman who spoke with an accent he didn't recognize.

"I'm Mrs. Jacobson," the first white woman introduced herself. "You must be tired. Nora will show you to a place to sleep. I am afraid you will have to stay there during the day, but Nora will bring you lunch and check on you from time to time."

"When do I leave?" Nathaniel asked.

"So newly arrived and so eager to leave," Mrs. Jacobson commented.

"I don't mean to sound ungrateful, ma'am," Nathaniel said.

"I know you don't. I will see to getting you a ferry across the river tonight. Then you will be a free man." The corners of her eyes, wrinkled with age, seemed to twinkle at him as she left the room. Free? Was it true?

"Finish up," Nora told him. "We can't have the governor comin' down and seein' you."

"The governor?" Nathaniel asked.

"The missus' son. We call him governor. Twice run for governor. Twice failed. I think he fancies hisself one anyway."

"He doesn't know about …?"

"It his momma's house. She run it. She let him have the appearance of runnin' it," Nora explained.

"Pay her no mind," the other servant said. "If he shows up, we will tell him you are a delivery boy come in for a bite before going on your way. He'll be none the wiser. I'm Isabelle," the white servant introduced herself. "He doesn't know the half of what goes on in his momma's home. She likes it that way." Both women laughed till a bell rang.

"Time to bring breakfast," Isabelle said as she picked up a tray and left.

Nora showed him into a small room in the basement with bare floors and a cot. "It not much, but you safe here. I check on you." Nathaniel thanked her for her kindness then stretched out on the cot, placing his knapsack with his worldly possessions under his head as a pillow. He wondered, would he ever see Cascade Falls again?

Chapter 19

Detroit – Present Day

Letty kept the immigration status of the Pinedas to herself, as advised by Walter. The only other person she told was Sara.

Walter had been surprised when Letty called him that afternoon. "I'm sorry to bother you on a Sunday, but I have a situation."

"What kind of situation?"

"Is there any chance you could meet me at Freedom House?"

"I have to finish something here, but can be there by four."

"That will work."

"This is the situation," Letty said as she took Walter through the house to the kitchen and the Pineda family. Derrick was sitting at a table playing a game with the children, laughing and smiling in a way she hadn't thought he was capable. She shook her head in surprise then explained the situation to Walter and waited for his response. He took her aside to another room to talk.

"Do you know what you are getting yourself into?"

"No. That's why I called you. I was hoping you could tell me."

"I don't know if I can help them. I'm not an immigration lawyer."

"But don't you know someone who is?"

"Most of my lawyer friends are corporate, but I'll check around. If ICE raids this place you might be charged with harboring illegals."

"Seems appropriate, doesn't it? For a place called Freedom House and former site of the Underground Railroad."

"Are you sure you want to do this?"

"I'm just helping out a family in need. What is there to think about?"

"Because that family can become another."

"I'll deal with that when and if I have to. One family at a time. Are you going to help me or not?" She should have known better than to expect him to understand. She was prepared to ask him to leave till he sighed.

"I'll see what I can do."

"Thank you. That's all I'm asking." Letty smiled to herself. She had won this one.

The Pineda family settled into Freedom House as if they had always lived there. Carlos made sure the doors were unlocked for classes and locked afterwards, kept the floor swept clean, and did odd jobs around the house. Rachel, his wife, busied herself in the kitchen, preparing food for her family which she shared with Letty. Somehow they came up with make-shift furniture for the rooms they occupied and pots and pans and utensils for the kitchen. Carlos worked odd jobs during the day to provide money for food. Rachel home-schooled the children, not wanting to take chances on their whereabouts being discovered through the school.

Letty invited the children to take part in the dance classes. Alberto wasn't interested, but Maryuri wanted to.

"Can I, Mamacita?"

"But you don't have proper clothes for dance classes."

"I'll find her some. She's more than welcome. No charge. I need the students," Letty told her.

"You should teach the traditional dance of my people," Rachel said.

"Can you show me?"

"Yes." Rachel did a simple dance step, a Honduran folk dance. "We are meztizos," she told Letty. "Mixed. Part Indian and part Spanish. When the Spaniards came, they conquered my people. My people, they went up into the mountains and hid. But even there, they found us. They could not wipe us out so we married. This is the dance of my people."

"Would you teach me?"

"It is simple. Come, Alberto and Maryuri will dance with you." Rachel taught her the steps as the children danced with her.

"We could offer a class, if you would teach it," Letty told her.

"Me? No. I can't do that."

"Sure you can. You can do it better than me. Do you think there are children who would like to learn?"

"Si, en mi familia. I could ask the families from my country. We could make it a fiesta. Food and dance."

"Sounds like a great idea. Let's do it." Letty was always ready for new ideas. She loved bringing in traditional dances from the many cultures that made up Detroit. She taught new dances each week at Sara's school, researching dances from the different cultures represented at the school. She was familiar with dances from Africa through her involvement with Alvin Ailey. While on break, she had travelled to Uganda with Shaunte who had friends working there as missionaries. Villagers would greet guests with a dance of welcome. Dance had been a regular part of life with each tribe having their own particular dance style. Dance wasn't meant to be a spectator sport. All were encouraged to join in. She loved the variety of dances, especially when they rolled their hip and stomach almost like a belly dancer. The kids at school had particularly liked the Luganda. They would spread their legs in a wide squat and wiggle, while other students banged drums. Through Rachel and her wider family, she was learning about traditional dances from Central America. She also hoped to incorporate dances from India and other Asian countries, as well as Native American dances. There was so much to learn and so much to teach. If only she could get the students and the funding.

When she expressed frustration with the low attendance at Freedom House classes, Sara suggested she go out into the highways and byways.

"Like in the Bible. When the guests invited to the wedding feast didn't show, the servants went out into the streets and invited people to come."

"They won't be interested in ballet and can't afford to pay for classes if they were."

"How do you know unless you try? Offer classes they would be interested in. Do introductory classes for free just to get people in the door. You can price the classes at a rate they can afford and offer scholarships to those who can't pay. Isn't that what you always wanted to do?"

"Yes, it is. But I need money to pull it off."

"You already have the building. You have some classes set up. Give it a try. If it works, we can write grants to get money to keep it going. If it works, the money will come."

"I wish I were as certain as you are," Letty said. Once she had said the same thing about Joy's Center for the Arts in Cascade Falls. But this was Detroit. And now she was the one who stood to lose everything if it failed.

"You aren't in this alone," Sara assured her putting her hand on Letty's arm. "Remember that, Letty. We are in this together." Letty wished she were as confident.

Chapter 20

Detroit – Present Day

When she had first talked to Walter about Freedom House, he had been supportive. He had even invited her to attend a local church with him.

"Come to Second Street Baptist. If you are looking for more information about the Underground Railroad, that's where you need to be. Lots of movers and shakers in the church. It would be good for you to get to know them. Second Street Baptist was instrumental in helping thousands of slaves to freedom. They have a museum and tours. Come with me this Sunday and check it out." It appeared to be the politically correct thing to do. She was not interested in being politically correct. She just wanted to dance and teach dance. But she could meet influential people who could help move Freedom House forward, so she had agreed.

Letty enjoyed the museum and the tour, mentally taking notes of ideas for Freedom House. Besides the tours, Second Street Baptist had an active church community. She liked that. She wanted some type of museum with the history of the house, but didn't want to turn the whole place into a monument to the past. She wanted a living, breathing house. She wanted to create new memories, new history. She had visions of children of all races, but especially those who had little economic opportunity, coming to Freedom House, participating in the arts.

When she talked to Walter about opening classes to the people from the streets and the neighborhood, he had been skeptical.

"You don't know the danger you might be putting yourself into," he told her.

"It's just kids."

"Kids grow up into big kids and get into trouble."

"This will help them stay out of trouble, give them something else to fill their time, a new perspective, a new chance they wouldn't ordinarily get."

"I'm not so sure about you putting yourself at risk like that. It's not the best neighborhood. You, being there at night. What kind of security do you have?"

"You're beginning to sound like my father, or worse, my mother. We have Carlos. He's all the security I need."

Walter found an immigration lawyer to look into Carlos and his family's situation. That was all the further he was involved. Letty sighed as she told Sara.

"What did you expect?" Sara asked her.

"I guess, I was hoping, maybe he would take the case himself."

"He's not an immigration lawyer."

"I know, but I thought, maybe he would be on board with this. Maybe even provide help for others."

"Letty. What are you talking about?"

"It's just, the Pineda family is just the tip of the iceberg. When it comes to immigrants needing help through the system, they are just one family of many. I've been thinking, maybe we could do more for them? There's a whole community here from Sudan. And other parts of Africa. You remember the Sudanese boys?"

"Yes, boy soldiers, boys ripped from their families, turned into soldiers."

"Boys, no older than your Gabe."

"A number of them came here to Michigan."

"With the help of our government. There are others who are fleeing inhumane conditions as well. I was thinking, maybe we could help them." Her brain was spinning with the possibility, all they could do.

"What about the Dance Studio?"

"I'm still doing that. We could do both. Think about it. Freedom House. If the abolitionists from the Civil War era were around today, what would they be doing?"

Sara paused and shook her head in reluctant agreement, "Maybe helping immigrants."

"Right. I know it's not an apples-to-apples comparison, slaves to immigrants. Still, it's the closest comparison I know. It involves loss of freedom and racism. What if we set up legal services in one of the rooms in the house? We have plenty of space. We won't be filling all of the rooms with artists."

"I guess we can talk to the board about it. You know, this will mean more work for you. Unpaid work."

"Bring it on." Letty could tell Sara wasn't onboard with the suggestion. It didn't matter. She was not to be deterred.

Chapter 21

Cascade Falls – Present Day

Ashley looked at the text from her aunt. Pastor Joe didn't waste any time.

"Ashley. It's been so long since we've had dinner, just the two of us. When are you available?"

Ashley didn't answer right away. She loved Aunt Kathleen, but really. She had been much more interesting before she married Pastor Joe. Then she had been the cool aunt, the one who had helped her through her mom's death. Now she was just as boring as everyone's mother or aunt.

She figured she couldn't put her off forever, so finally texted back. "How about Friday?" She hated giving up her Friday night, but with going to the dance studio every night after school, it was the only free night she had. That or Saturday. She figured they could go out to eat then she could dump her aunt to go to the basketball game at school. Not that she was that much into sports. She liked to make fun of the cheerleaders. But Caleb was playing, and she did like him.

"Great!" Aunt Kathleen texted back. "Where do you want to go? Burgers? Pizza?"

"You know I'm vegan, right?"

"How about a veggie pizza?"

They decided on a local restaurant where Ashley could get salad and Aunt Kathleen her burger.

Aunt Kathleen worked her way through all of the usual small talk, trying to make conversation. Ashley wasn't cooperating.

"Why is this so hard, Ashley? We used to talk about everything," Aunt Kathleen finally said.

"Because I've grown up. I've changed."

"I'd like to think, no matter how grown up you become, we would always have something to talk about."

"Aunt Kathleen, I know what this is about. Why don't you just get to it?" Ashley sipped her water. "I know Pastor Joe told you about our conversation. That's why you wanted to go out, isn't it?"

"It's not the only reason. I miss our monthly dinners." Aunt Kathleen looked relieved when their waitress arrived with the burger and salad. Ashley watched as her aunt took a big bite. Ketchup and mustard oozed out the sides. To think, there was a time when Ashley would have had a burger equally as big and sloppy. That was before she became a vegan. To think, there actually was a time when she had believed in God. Yes, she had grown-up.

Ashley waited for her aunt to put her burger down before picking up the conversation.

"Aunt Kathleen, I know you are here because Pastor Joe told you I'm an atheist." Her aunt almost choked on the food that remained in her mouth. "It's okay. I know what I'm doing. I thought this out before deciding. It's not some rash decision I made without thinking."

Aunt Kathleen swallowed her food and took a drink of water. "It's just, do you really understand what you have decided? All of the implications? It's lonely going through life without a belief system and a community. I ought to know. I did it for the first forty years of my life."

"I have a belief system, Aunt Kathleen. And people who think like me, an online community."

"I just don't want you to go aimlessly through life, not caring for anyone but yourself, the way I did."

"I'm not like you, Aunt Kathleen. I have a goal for life. Don't worry. I'll be okay."

"I wish I could believe that," her aunt said.

"Believe what you will, Aunt Kathleen. And I'll believe what I will." That settled it as far as she was concerned. Time to ditch her aunt and go to the game.

Chapter 22

Detroit – Present Day

Walter's church just wasn't right for her. She didn't know why, didn't know what it was about the church. After taking her to Second Baptist Church that one Sunday, Walter had invited her to attend his church with him, another Baptist church. The people were friendly enough, the preacher dynamic, as well as the music.

Walter had introduced her to his friends, other lawyers and professionals. They gave the appearance of being interested in what she was doing at Freedom House, but that was it. Was it possible that they were too black and middle-class for her? Did that even make sense? Her home church in Cascade Falls had been predominantly black, but not as middle-class, though you wouldn't know it from how church members dressed. No matter how little they had, everyone dressed for church at Cascade Falls AME. Not like the church services she had attended while in college. There it was come as you are. Students routinely wore jeans to church, something unheard of in her home church.

But she knew the members of Cascade Falls AME, knew her cousins and their friends, knew their families were far from middle-class. She knew they were among the families helped by regular collections of donated food and money. She also knew that some of her cousins resented her because she knew.

"Hmmmph," she remembered her cousin Latrese, her lips curled into a snarl, scraping her leg with her foot, snagging her nylons and leaving mud on her new dress shoes. She remembered it as well as if it were yesterday. She had been in sixth grade and delighted with the new shoes her mom had bought her, fancy shoes, her first heels. She couldn't wait to show them off, until her cousin made her want to hide them in her closet.

"Leticia, what happened to your new shoes?" her mother had questioned when she saw the mud on them.

"Sorry, Mama." Letty hadn't bothered to explain. She let her mother draw her own conclusion rather than rat out her cousin.

"That girl, can't give her anything nice," her mother had commented to her friend.

Only her cousin Martell had understood and befriended her.

"Pay them no mind. They're just jealous. It's not your fault you're rich."

"I'm not rich," Letty had protested.

"Look around you, girl. You're rich. You have a nice home in the suburbs. Your parents have two cars, ones that aren't constantly in need of repair, you always have food on the table and you wear designer clothes. If that's not rich, I don't know what is."

Slowly, Letty came to realize what Martell was saying was true. It hadn't made a difference when she was younger. It never occurred to her that her cousins didn't have everything she had. Wasn't everyone's family like hers? As she came to realize that wasn't true, she found herself spending less time with her cousins and more time with her friends from school. Friends that she had more in common with, friends from other middle-class families. White friends that took music lessons, dance lessons. Friends that didn't leave her feeling guilty for something over which she had no control. Still, she didn't forget her cousins. They remained, pushed temporarily out of her mind, but present in the background.

Maybe she just didn't know the members of Walter's church well enough yet. Maybe if she knew them, she would realize that it was a similar economic mix to her home church. Still, she had little inclination to get to know them. Something was missing. Letty wasn't sure what she was looking for. Maybe she would know it when she found it.

She had also gone out with Walter numerous times, sometimes to night clubs like the first one she had met him at, other times to the ballet or symphony.

"Do you miss it?" Walter asked her after each ballet performance.

"Yes, and no. I do miss it, but I like what I'm doing. I was ready for a change when I left."

Letty enjoyed going out to eat at a nice restaurant then going to the symphony or ballet. Who would have thought there were such opportunities in Detroit? The Detroit featured in most news articles was the Detroit of 8 Mile and rapper Eminem, or the Detroit of the infamous riots of the 1960s. Even though there was change afoot to remake Detroit, it was hard to break out of a long history.

She also loved what she was doing at Freedom House, but felt guilty at times for enjoying opportunities the people from the neighborhood didn't have. Felt guilty about the money spent on nights out, even though it wasn't her money.

"A girl could get used to this," she commented after their last date.

"That's what I'm hoping," Walter said as he kissed her.

"That's not the way I meant it."

"Then what do you mean?"

"It's not necessarily a good thing."

"What are you talking about?" Walter pulled back.

"Not you, not us. I mean, the nights out, the fancy restaurants."

"What's wrong with that? I thought you enjoyed going to the ballet and symphony."

"I do. It's just …" — how could she explain it to him when she didn't understand it herself? "It's not everything."

"Who said it was everything?"

"No, I mean, I like it. It would be far too easy to live in this world of privilege and forget all those who have so little."

"Small chance of you ever doing that. Not with your work at Freedom House."

"And there's that. I thought you supported what I'm doing at Freedom House."

Walter sighed. "So it's this again. I thought you were building a dance studio and center for the arts and maybe a historical museum on the Underground Railroad. Instead you insist on inviting in all kinds of people from the street, illegals. Do you have any idea what you are doing?

"Now you sound like my board of directors."

"If I do, then maybe you need to listen to them." Walter tried to wrap her in his arms. "Leticia, I'm worried about your safety. You can still make an impact on people's lives without putting your own in jeopardy."

Letty pulled away from him. "I didn't come here to play it safe. I came here to make a difference, one dancer at a time. One person at a time. Those people who opened their doors to runaway slaves almost two hundred years ago weren't playing it safe. They didn't put their own safety or the safety of their family above the safety of those individuals whose lives were in danger. Why should I?"

"I'm just suggesting that maybe you've lost your way. You're a dancer, not an abolitionist or a radical."

"Can't I be both?" Letty faced him. She felt her heart blazing with a passion she wasn't aware she had.

"Can you? Can you and be true to yourself?"

"I'm certainly going to try." Letty stormed off to her apartment over Sara's garage, leaving Walter standing there. Who was he to try to tell her who she was? She turned around after safely unlocking her door and closing it behind her and looked out the window to see if he was still there. He was. Even when angry, he waited to make sure she got home and inside safely. She didn't know why she was so angry. She just was.

Chapter 23

Kathleen came home from dinner with Ashley, threw her purse on the coffee table and sat down on the couch next to him. Joe waited for her to break the silence.

"Aren't you going to ask me how it went?" Kathleen asked.

"Clearly not good. What happened?"

"Well, I didn't convince her."

"Ashley's pretty strong-willed. What did you think would happen?"

"I didn't think I would be able to change her mind. I just wanted to keep the door open."

"Did you do that?"

"I doubt it." She sat sideways in order to face him. "I can't believe you left it up to her to decide."

Joe looked at his wife. Was he hearing right?

"Are you really trying to pin this on me? You, more than anyone, should recognize how crazy that is. You know Ashley. Like anyone could force her to believe anything she didn't want to believe."

"Ashley's too young to make such an important decision."

"Is she? And how am I to keep her from exercising her free will?"

"Just tell her no. There is a God. No question about it."

"Kathleen, who am I to take away the free will God gave her?" He couldn't believe what he was hearing. What was this woman saying? Wasn't she the same person who only started attending church a few years ago? "If this were anyone else besides Ashley, you would be supporting their right to their own opinion."

"I don't care. Make it happen. You're a minister and her uncle. Tell her."

"And what good would that do? I can tell her whatever I want. Doesn't mean she will listen." Joe continued to shake his head in disbelief.

"Tell her she'll burn in hell if she doesn't believe."

"Come on, Kathleen. You don't really believe that. Do you think scare tactics will get her to change her mind? Would they have worked with you when you were her age?" Joe stared straight into her eyes. What was going on in that head of hers?

"But, as messed up as I was, I still believed in God. I just never gave God any thought back then. Didn't mean I didn't believe." Kathleen thrust her lower lip forward in a pout and turned away, refusing to meet his gaze.

"What's worse? To not believe in God but still live a moral life, or believe in God but act like God doesn't exist?" He knew he had her there. Kathleen refused to admit it. Instead she took a different tact, facing him.

"I don't know about this free will thing. I think God made a mistake, giving humans free will. Look at where free will has gotten us. Wars, holocausts, violence, abuse. If we didn't have free will, we would be living according to God's plan for us. We wouldn't be free to mess up, make mistakes or deny God's existence."

"We would be back in the garden."

"Right, where we were living in accordance with God's will, walking with God."

"And yet, Adam and Even freely chose to eat the apple."

"So, it's their fault." Kathleen seemed happy to access blame.

"Is it their fault, or God's fault?"

"God's fault?"

"Yes, for giving them the ability to choose in the first place."

Kathleen slouched and pulled further away from him. "How did we get here in the first place?"

"We were talking about Ashley."

"Oh, yeah, that. Well, I think God shouldn't give us free will until we are old enough to make good decisions. Ashley's too young to make such a decision."

"And yet the fact that she can think and reason enough to even ask the question, isn't that a sign that she is old enough to make a decision, however much you may disagree with that decision?"

"I think God has some explaining to do. I mean to ask him about this when I see him."

Joe shook his head and smiled at this. "You won't be the first or the last. Theologians have struggled over the question of free will for centuries."

"You'd think they would have figured it out by now."

"You think?"

"Yes, why would God give us a question that has no answer?"

"Maybe to keep us asking." Joe smiled again. His wife definitely knew how to keep him on his toes.

"Well, I think the system stinks."

"You talk to God about that."

"I will."

"And when you do, put in a good word for me."

"Always." Kathleen smiled and slid over closer to him.

"And now you know how God must feel as we make poor choices. How helpless our all-powerful God is before our free will, our poor choices." Kathleen slipped under his arm as he spoke. "When people ask how God can allow bad things to happen, I ask, how can we people allow evil to happen? God gave us free will. That means we can choose for or against God. We can choose evil over good."

"Then God is to blame for giving us free will in the first place."

"Maybe, but if we didn't have free will, we wouldn't be able to freely choose to love God. What value is love if not freely given? Is it even possible to love if there is no freedom to choose?"

Kathleen curled up further under his arm. "Joe, what is it about these girls? Why are they so determined to ruin their lives?"

"So, we aren't just talking about Ashley?"

"No, I'm talking about Ashley and Stephanie. Why don't they listen to reason?" Kathleen pulled away from him and faced him as she spoke.

"Did you listen to reason when you were their age?"

"No. That's why I'm so worried. I don't want them to spend years of their life adrift with no anchor, no support, like I did."

"They aren't you, Kathleen. Neither Stephanie nor Ashley are you. They have to make their own mistakes. All we can do is stand ready to support them when they fall." Joe pulled Kathleen back under his arm.

"You've said, you wish you could have more kids, maybe girls. Well, now you know what it's like to be a mother of girls."

"That so? You know what? It's over-rated," Kathleen said as she burrowed further into the shelter of his arm.

Chapter 24

Cascade Falls – 1853

Josiah had not wanted to send his grandson on such a long journey but he had no one else to send and Nathaniel had to go immediately. The youth was but a boy of fifteen. Josiah knew he could not manage such a long journey, not at his age, and his son Edward was gone overnight.

"I will be fine, Grandpa," Wesley had insisted.

"You come straight home," his ma told him.

"Yes, Ma."

"No straying off the path, no stopping on the way."

"The boy knows what he is doing," Josiah stepped in to defend his grandson.

"I just wish Edward was here to go," his daughter-in-law said. "Or anyone else."

"He will be fine," Josiah insisted. Edward was away for the night, attending meetings in the Capital. He ran the local newspaper and was covering what was happening in the legislature. He wouldn't get home till later the next day.

"When will all of this be over," Elizabeth said as she turned towards the house.

"Not till the South sees reason." Josiah knew his daughter-in-law was a supporter of freeing the slaves. Her beliefs faltered when it affected the safety of her family. She was a reluctant participant in the family activities.

"I love Edward, and I want to be supportive …" she had told Josiah years ago. "But …" He knew where she drew the line. Still, she had a kind heart, must have to have married his son. She had known what she was getting into when she married into the family. It was no secret that they were staunch abolitionists. Elizabeth accepted this, but she didn't embrace it, even when families with small children passed through their home. Josiah had thought that would convert her, but it didn't. Even when she heard tales of atrocities, slaves beaten, children abused, families separated, sold like cattle. She couldn't get past her fear for her own family. At least she didn't interfere with their work.

He knew she wouldn't sleep well while Wesley was away, would not be able to rest until he was home again. That was the price they paid, one of the prices.

The town was in uproar that morning when Josiah got to his law office. Nathaniel's master had come to the court house and presented his documents. He wanted his property and he wanted it now. Under the Fugitive Slave Act, they were required to help him. Nathaniel's master was threatening lawsuits for aiding and abetting a runaway. The court officers went into deliberations. Meanwhile, outside the courthouse, a crowd was gathering. Other deliberations were taking place. Josiah had summoned all of the local members of the Underground Railroad. Farmers left their fields, jumped on horseback and headed into town. There they could be seen discussing what course of action to take. Josiah met them outside the courthouse and suggested they go across the street to the church.

"What can he do? Nathaniel is already gone? We can't give him what we don't have." Words flew about the church sanctuary.

"He can sue us for loss of property. We can be thrown in jail for aiding and abetting a runaway slave. He can try to take down the railroad," Josiah explained.

"He can't do that, can he?"

"He can try, and make our lives miserable in the process."

"What are we to do then?" they deliberated for a while till someone came up with a plan.

"What if we pay for Nathaniel? Pay his master a fair rate for his freedom?" They agreed on this plan then walked back across the street to the courthouse where Josiah presented the proposal.

"He was trained as a barber, at my expense," Nathaniel's owner insisted. "I couldn't sell him for any less than ..." he paused as he did some figuring in his head. "One thousand dollars." There were gasps throughout the courtroom. How could they come up with that much money? Who had that kind of money? They were just simple farmers. They barely made $250 in one year.

"Now Mr. Wright, you know that you were going to make an example of this man once you got him home," Josiah said.

"How do you know that? Barbers are worth money. Why would I throw away so much money just to make a point? And if I did, it is my right. He is my property and I can do with him what I want."

"Well, one thousand dollars is a heap of money. Let me confer with my colleagues." Josiah turned around to speak to the men gathered.

"We can't come up with one thousand dollars."

"How much do you think we can get?" Josiah asked. They talked amongst themselves.

"If we all chip in, we can get seven hundred dollars," the spokesman said for the group.

"That will have to do," Josiah said, then turned back to the judge. "Your honor, we are willing to offer six hundred dollars for the slave, Nathaniel Wright."

"Six hundred dollars. I can't sell him for that. I can't sell him for less than eight hundred dollars. Even with that I'd be taking a loss," Mr. Wright said.

"Seven hundred," Josiah said.

"No less than seven hundred and fifty," Mr. Wright insisted.

"We accept," Josiah said. The crowd gasped again. So much money. "I will draw up the paperwork and you will have your money tomorrow. We want Nathaniel Wright's papers, free and clear."

"I will make up any shortage," Josiah assured the men as they gathered the payment. By the next afternoon, the abolitionists of Cascade Falls had purchased a slave.

"Now we just have to get Nathaniel back so we can set him free," Josiah said.

Chapter 25

Detroit – Present Day

Letty nervously prepared for the next board meeting. She was going to present her proposal for the legal service office. The meeting was being held during the lunch hour at Derrick's office building to make it easier for him to attend.

"What do you think? Do you think they will be okay with it?" she had asked Sara beforehand.

"I don't know. It's not exactly in our mission or how we saw Freedom House operating."

"But it's Freedom House. Perhaps you chose the name, and now the house is choosing its mission."

Letty figured she had Sara and Derrick on her side. If only she could get the rest of the board to agree.

"I thought we were going to focus on the arts, helping struggling artists?" were the first words of resistance. Letty was prepared for them.

"We can still do that. We aren't talking about changing the mission. This isn't the whole scope of the building, just one aspect, one way to be of service, one way to live up to the name 'Freedom House'."

Letty had expected to meet resistance to her proposal, just not as much as she did.

Sara didn't even back her up. That left Derrick in support of her.

"Letty, do you know what you are getting yourself into?" the board chair questioned her. "What do you know about setting up a legal services office?"

"The idea is that the lawyers will put it all together," Letty explained.

"But that's not how your proposal reads."

"I thought the idea was to have like-minded non-profits set up office in the building and pay rent to help offset the costs of operating the building."

"Yes, but this isn't an established non-profit. If you had a group of lawyers who were committed to this and already had funding who were looking for a space, that would be different."

"I have some lawyers on board."

"But who is going to make it happen, Letty? Do you know how hard it is to get a non-profit off the ground? Where will the funding come from?" the chair asked.

"Grants, donations."

"And how are they going to get those grants and donations?"

"I can help."

"That's precisely the problem. The dance studio is hardly up and running. How are you going to make this happen? How will you find the time?"

"Won't you help?" Letty looked around the table then settled on Sara, expecting her to agree. Sara remained silent.

"Letty," the board chair continued. "If you had a group of lawyers who wanted to open an office in Freedom House, that would be different. I'm not opposed to the idea, just to you giving too much of your time to it."

"But if that's what I want to do?"

"We can't tell you what to do with your free time. As long as it doesn't interfere with doing what you came here to do." The chair looked around the table and asked for further discussion. There being none, she moved onto the next agenda item. Letty sat quietly through the rest of the meeting, only speaking when directly asked a question.

"What happened in there?" Letty asked Sara after everyone had cleared out but the two of them. "I thought you had my back?"

"Letty, I think they were making sense. Don't you think you are stretching yourself too thin?"

"But peoples' lives are at stake."

"You can't solve all the world's problems."

"I know, but what about the ones I can."

"Are those really your problems to solve, Letty?"

"What do you mean?"

"Think about it. You came here to open a dance studio and a Center for the Arts. How much time are you actually spending on your art, on dancing?"

"I'm teaching classes."

"And ..."

"And what? I have to spend time marketing, trying to bring in new students, set up the business end of the dance studio. You know, it's not all about dancing. It's a business."

"And now you want to set up another business. Is that how you really want to spend your time?" Sara waited for Letty to respond. When she didn't, Sara added, "Or is it just a way to run away from what you really want to do? A distraction from what you are meant to do?"

"What are you talking about?"

"I'm talking about ... ever since I started trying to set up this Center for the Arts, I've had no time for my own art work. All of my free time has been spent on helping you with the dance studio and the art center. I've been asking myself why. Is it my way of avoiding the hard work, discouragement and frustration that is part of making it as an artist, part of any artistic career? I know you don't have as many students and classes as you would like, but are you really called to start something new, an entirely new direction, however worthy it may be? Or are you called to persevere in what you started? Are you called to teach dance or to run a non-profit?"

"Why does this conversation seem so familiar?" Letty didn't wait for Sara to respond. "It's a conversation I've had most of my life, with myself. All those years dancing, studying dance, teaching dance in Cascade Falls while pursuing a degree in social work. The conversation I've had with my mother who wanted me to go into social work, like her. The conversation I thought I had put to rest when

I went away to dance with Alvin Ailey. Back then, I had made a choice to dance. Here I am, six years later, still dealing with the same questions." Letty shook her head as the words poured out.

"You know, I love dancing, loved dancing with Alvin Ailey. But I came back here because it just wasn't enough for me, not enough for a lifetime. I guess I keep thinking I can have it all. I want to be able to dance, to teach dance, but I also want to help others, put my social work background to use."

"And you think you aren't helping by teaching?"

"No, it is helping, just not enough. I don't see enough results. There are so many pressing needs out there. I keep thinking about how my ancestors were runaway slaves. The hardships they experienced in order to make it here, to forge a new life for themselves. And I think about the people who risked their lives to save them, the people along the stations of the Underground Railroad. I feel like I owe it to them."

"What do you owe them?"

"To do the same for others."

"Maybe what you owe them is to simply live the freedom they fought for. They fought for the right to marry the person they chose, raise a family, buy a home, choose a profession. All of these freedoms we take for granted. Maybe you honor them most by making use of the freedoms. The freedom to do what you love. If what you love is dance and teaching others to dance, then do it. Exercise your freedom."

"But is it enough? Am I making enough of a difference?"

Sara paused before answering. "Think about Joy. Her life was dedicated to dance. To dance and her family and her students. Was that enough? Did she make enough of a difference? In her short life, I believe she had an impact."

"Yes, she did. There's no question of that."

"Then why do you think you aren't doing enough in following in her footsteps?"

"I don't know." Letty shook her head and slouched her shoulders.

"Think about it," Sara said.

Letty's phone rang. She looked at it, unsure who the caller was. She didn't recognize the number but decided to take the call anyway.

"Leticia?" she heard the Spanish version of her name.

"Rachel? What's wrong?"

"Come quick. ICE. They are here. They come to take us."

"But how?" Letty started then shook her head. "Never mind, I'll be right there." Letty clicked off her phoned.

"What's wrong?" Sara asked.

"That was Rachel," Letty said as she picked up her purse.

"How did she call?"

"I don't know. Must have borrowed a phone from someone." Rachel was opening the dance studio for her while she was at the board meeting. "ICE is there. I've got to get to the dance studio as soon as possible, before they take them." Letty was already out of the boardroom.

"Wait. I'll drive." Sara followed after her. Letty didn't argue. Derrick saw them rushing out and called after them.

"What's going on?"

"ICE," Letty said.

"Janet, take my calls," Derrick said to his secretary then grabbed his suit jacket and followed after them. "Wait for me." He caught the door of the elevator.

"I can't believe this is happening," Letty kept saying. "They were supposed to be considered for asylum, not being deported. Their lawyer was doing all the legal work. How could this happen?" Letty called the lawyer assigned to their case and told him what was happening.

"He's going to meet us there," she said as the elevator came to a stop. She tried to remain calm as Sara drove to Freedom House. "This is all my fault."

"How is that?" Sara asked.

"I insisted on them filing paperwork with the department of immigration to obtain legal status. If I hadn't insisted, ICE never would have known where they were staying."

"ICE could have found out anyway. You did what you believed to be right," Derrick told her from the back seat. Sara reached over and squeezed Letty's hand for a moment to reassure her. Letty didn't respond.

Sara dropped Letty and Derrick off at Freedom House then looked for a parking place.

Letty pushed her way through the young dancers being dropped off by their parents for class, not waiting for Derrick to catch up with her. Her students gathered around outside the door to the ballroom where classes were held, watching what was going on.

ICE agents had Rachel and her two children in their custody. They kept asking Rachel where her husband was.

Letty went up to the ICE agent who appeared to be in charge. "What are you doing? Release this woman and her children. They haven't done anything wrong."

"Who are you?" the agent asked.

"I run this dance studio."

"Back off or you will be charged with interfering with an officer in the exercise of his duty as well as harboring illegals."

"This woman has applied for asylum." Derrick caught up with Letty.

"She'll have to go back to her country and go through the proper channels."

"If she does, she and her children may be killed before being re-admitted," Letty said.

"Look, lady, I don't create the laws. I just enforce them. If you have a problem with it, get a lawyer."

At that point, Andrew, the Pinedas' lawyer arrived, followed by Sara.

"I do have a lawyer. He's here," Letty pointed at Andrew as he came forward.

Andrew shook the agent's hand as he introduced himself.

"Where are you taking my clients?" he asked.

"Into custody."

"Do you realize they are seeking asylum?"

"Tell that to the judge. For now, I've got orders to bring them in." The man handed Andrew the papers. Andrew looked them over then handed them back. "We are just waiting for the husband. Do you know where he is?" Andrew shook his head no and looked at Letty.

"I don't know," Letty said. "He does odd jobs to provide for his family. He could be anywhere." She turned to Rachel. "Rachel, do you know where Carlos is working today?"

"No," she answered.

"Well, when he shows up, let him know it will go better for him if he turns himself in," the agent handed Letty his card then ordered the two other agents to take the family. Alberto started to resist when his mother said no.

"We have to go with these men," she told him, looking first to the lawyer then to Letty for confirmation.

"That's right, son," Andrew said. "I'll follow and see what I can do," he reassured them.

"Can I come with you?" Derrick asked. When Andrew nodded his head yes, he told Letty he would let her know what was happening. "I think you've got a class to teach."

The group of parents and students stood watching as the family was taken away.

"Where are they taking Maryuri?" a little girl from the class asked. Letty got down on her knees to talk to her.

"Maryuri will be okay," she assured her. "She's with her mother."

"Is there anything we can do to help?" one of the mothers asked.

"I'll let you know," Letty told her. "Now it's time to dance. No more long faces. I'll be right there." Letty handed her phone to Sara as she went to get her leotard on. "Hold onto this in case someone calls while I'm teaching."

Chapter 26

Detroit – Present Day

Derrick called in between classes and let her know Rachel and her children were being held in the detention center. When Carlos came home, Letty told him what had happened. He called Andrew and, based on his recommendation, joined his wife and children in detention.

When Letty got home that night, she saw Walter had called twice. She didn't return his calls. She answered the knocks on her door and let Sara in with the tray of food she was holding.

"I thought maybe you could use a meal."

"Not now, Sara."

"You okay? You want to talk?"

"What's there to talk about? Rachel and her family are in detention, awaiting deportation back to Honduras. It's my fault. Who am I to think I can help anyone?"

"Letty, chances are they would have been caught by ICE sooner or later. At least now they have a lawyer working for them."

Letty remained silent.

"Walter called me. He's worried about you. Said you aren't returning his calls."

"If I wanted to talk to him, I would have returned his call."

"What should I tell him if he calls again?"

"Tell him whatever you want to tell him."

"Okay. Are you sure you are okay?"

"No, I'm not okay, but there's nothing you can do. Go back to your family."

Sara paused as if going to say something, then thought better of it and let herself out.

Letty let the food Sara brought grow cold on the plate. What a fool she had been, thinking she could help Carlos and Rachel. Her mind raced. What could she do? She sat and stared into darkness.

When she got up, she dumped the food into the garbage, then went to bed. Her phone rang again. She ignored it like all the other calls, but decided to check who had called in case Derrick had more news for her. A number she hadn't seen for months, not since moving back to Michigan, glared at her in the darkened room. James. She went to voice mail and listened to the deep, full throated voice, coming out of her phone.

"Hey, baby. Been thinking about you. I've got some business in Detroit this weekend. Would love to see you. Maybe dinner and a show. Call me."

Call him? Why him? Why now? Why when everything feels like it is falling apart around her, she gets this call from her past? A siren song calling her back to what she knew in New York? Now she had another reason to toss and turn all night.

Chapter 27

Detroit – Present Day

Letty didn't respond to Walter's or James' calls. She didn't know what she wanted and until she did, she thought it was better to not talk to either of them. Walter would just tell her he had warned her about this. James … James was a whole other story. A story she thought she had forgotten and left behind when she had moved. A story that she had thought was over. Was this an epilogue? Or a new chapter? Why was this part of her life coming back by way of an attractive six-foot two man with a sultry voice? A voice she found hard to resist. And what made matters worse, she couldn't even talk to Sara about this. After what had felt like a betrayal at the board meeting, she didn't know who she could trust.

James called every day that week. She persisted in her refusal to take his calls. His last message was, "Babe, I understand why you don't want to take my call, but I would really like to see you this weekend. I've made reservations for two at Iridescence for nine o'clock. Meet me there. I'll be the one with the sad puppy-dog look on my face and flowers."

Letty didn't know what she was going to do until Friday night, and even then she was not sure. She looked through the restaurant to where James sat alone, scanning his phone. She almost turned around and left, but he saw her. Letty took a deep breath and walked to his table. James stood up, took her hand and kissed her on the cheek.

"Now, that's what I'm talking about," he said as he looked her up and down before she sat down. "Grace in motion. I'm so glad you came." Letty had agonized about what dress to wear. She hadn't wanted to give the wrong message. She had been torn between wearing her little black dress, classic and fitting for any occasion, or her deep red dress. She had opted for the red one. Perhaps she should have gone with black.

James filled her in on all that she had been missing in New York, especially the latest gossip from Alvin Ailey.

"And what about Kylie?" Letty asked.

"Oh, baby. She was a mistake. It was just a fling. She wasn't you. I've been missing you."

"But not enough to call me before this?"

"And say what?"

"You think about it. Think about how we had ended. That should give you a clue."

"Say I'm sorry? That I was wrong? That you are the only one for me?"

"That would be a start." Letty laughed as she heard the words. She knew how insincere the words were, still it was nice to hear them.

"You know that's not me. I'm not a one-woman man. However, if I ever were to be one, you just might be the one." James curled the corner of his lips into a smile and raised his glass to her.

Letty laughed again. "You know that the only reason you called me was because you were going to be in Detroit and you hate to eat alone."

"That too. But I do miss you."

"And I miss this," Letty said. "Talking about New York, old friends, the night life."

"Are you ready to come back?"

"Are you giving me a reason to come back?"

"Not me, but there's still an opening at Alvin Ailey for you. You know how dancers come and go. You could get your place back, if you want it."

"If I want it," Letty rephrased his words. "That is the question." She wasn't sure what she wanted.

They went clubbing after dinner, ending up at the same nightclub where Letty had met Walter that night months ago.

It came as no surprise when she saw Walter with another woman on his arm. She introduced James to Walter.

"Any friend of Letty's is a friend of mine," Walter said. Letty heard the touch of insincerity in his voice.

"Who is your friend?" Letty asked him.

"Oh, this is Marjorie. She works at the firm with me."

"Another lawyer?"

"Yes," Walter said. "Marjorie, you don't mind if I talk to Letty for a minute. James, I need to borrow your date," he said, leaving the two of them together as he slipped his arm around Letty's waist and guided her away.

"You haven't returned my calls," he started. "Why?"

"I've been busy."

"I see that," Walter said, looking over at James as he talked to Marjorie.

"He's just a friend from New York. He's in town for business. Asked me to show him around." Letty glanced at Marjorie. "And what about your date?"

"Just a friend from work. I wanted to go out and you weren't returning my calls."

"Hey, that's okay. We never said we were exclusive. If you'll excuse me, I have to get back to my date."

"Letty, I heard about the Pineda family. I've been worried about you." Walter put his hand on her arm to stop her. "Did I do something wrong? What's going on?"

"Everything okay?" James approached with two flutes of champagnes. "Marjorie went to the ladies' room," he explained as he eyed Walter's hand. Walter let go of Letty's arm.

"No, nothing's wrong. I guess I better be looking for my date," Walter excused himself.

"What's going on?" James asked as he handed Letty the champagne. Letty accepted it even though she had already had her glass of white wine.

"Nothing," Letty told him as she took a sip. "Nothing at all."

"That's not what it looked like to me."

"Then maybe there's something wrong with your eyesight."

"I'm just trying to assess the competition." James cocked his head and clinked his champagne glass against hers.

"It isn't a competition," Letty stated. She glanced over at Walter as she continued to sip her champagne.

Chapter 28

Cascade Falls – Present Day

Ashley was sitting on her bed and peering into her phone, listening to music through headphones when she was hit by something soft. Now what? Ashley jumped. There on her bed was a pair of dirty socks, balled together into a weapon.

"Grace!" She pulled her headphones off and yelled at the head that had surfaced under the trap door that led to her attic bedroom.

"Dinner's ready," Grace said, then popped her head back to safety under the floor.

"I'm not hungry," Ashley said.

"You tell that to Dad and Ava," Grace retorted. Ashley heard her thump down the ladder and head back downstairs. She climbed off her bed and prepared to make the obligatory descent to join her family for dinner.

"Did you tell Ashley?" she heard her dad ask Grace.

"She says she's not hungry," Grace answered. Her dad sighed at this.

"I'll get her," he said as Ashley came through the door. "Good. Time for dinner." Ava brought in a plate of pork chops, followed by Jacob with the mashed potatoes. "Ashley, you go get the green beans," he told her.

"Ugh, pork chops. You know I don't eat meat," Ashley said as she made her way into the kitchen.

"You can eat potatoes, green beans and salad," Ava told her as she followed Ashley back into the kitchen to get tongs for the salad.

"I don't know why I have to sit at the table while you eat meat," Ashley complained as she carried in the bowl of green beans.

"Because we are a family and that's what families do," her dad insisted. "Now everyone sit down so we can say grace."

"Grace," Jacob said.

"Ha ha," Grace responded.

"How childish," Ashley said. She didn't know why Jacob always found this so funny. "How long do I have to put up with this?"

Her dad shook his head, ignored the question then waited for silence before reaching out to take Ava's hand on one side, Grace's on the other and praying.

Dishes were passed around and everyone was occupied with food.

"So, how was your day?" Her dad asked as he did every night. He waited for an answer, knowing that no one would say anything without coaxing. Ashley wondered why he even bothered.

"Fine," Ashley stated when no one answered. She finished off her last bite of salad and put down her fork. "Can I go now?"

"Actually, your stepmother and I have something to talk to you about after dishes are done," her dad said.

Here it comes, Ashley thought as she prepared herself for the inevitable.

Dale had been debating how best to approach Ashley. Joe had cautioned against overreacting.

"How are we to react when our daughter rejects all that we believe, all we hold dear?" Ava had asked him when he told her about his conversation with Joe.

"Not like that," Dale told her. Ava was Ashley's stepmother, but she had been the only mother Ashley had known for the past five years. Even given that, Dale knew Ava still walked on egg shells where Ashley was concerned. That would not have been the case with Joy, Ashley's mother. Joy would have known just what to say to handle this latest crisis with their oldest daughter. Or, at least, he thought so.

"It's as if she's going out of her way to be difficult," Ava stated.

"Maybe, or maybe this is the journey she needs to make. We can't force her to believe what we believe."

"I guess not. Will it ever get easy where that girl is concerned?"

"I don't know." Dale remembered another headstrong girl who had forged her own path, his sister. His mother had had all she could handle with Kathleen. Look how long it took for her to come around. He hoped it wouldn't be the same for Ashley.

They had been able to come to something of an understanding with Ashley. She agreed to continue to go to church on Sundays and holidays but they didn't push anything more than that.

"As long as you are living under our roof, you will go to church. You don't have to participate. You don't have to go to youth groups or other church activities, but you will go to church with us as a family because that's what we do. That's part of being in this family," Dale had told her.

"Okay. As long as I'm living with you," Ashley had agreed. Dale was afraid to ask what the wheels clicking in her head were telling her. He decided to leave well enough alone At least she was doing what they had told her to do. No argument. No pouting. He knew she was up to something, but was afraid to go there for fear of what he might discover.

Chapter 29

Ontario, Canada - 1853

Letty didn't know why ma and Sarai stopped just over the border in Ontario, Canada, rather than go any further. Perhaps they were just tired. Or maybe they dreamed of returning to the country they had fled. Surely there was no love for this country that had deprived them of their freedom, but there was love for the people they had left behind. Perhaps Ma was holding onto the hope that one day Daddy would cross that river and she wanted to be waiting for him.

Letty didn't know, but what she did know was that she was tired of running. She had been ready to put her feet to rest anywhere. This place seemed as good as the next. She did like its proximity to the state of Michigan. She liked the green patchwork of land and lakes she had seen, when not confined inside a wagon or traveling at night. She missed her daddy, but she didn't miss the plantation or the life she had led there. She had left friends behind, but found new friends, new family on their journey and now in this colony of free blacks and escaped slaves. New family like Sarai, whom she called aunt. Sarai was not that much older than her. Eight years if they reckoned right. Neither knew the day or year of their birth but had something of a recollection of how old they were. Birthdays weren't celebrated in slavery. Every day was but another day of servitude.

They celebrated Christmas, as much as they could. Ma used to try to make it special. Her mistress was moved to generosity by the season and usually gave the servants a ham and oranges and maple syrup candies for the children. Ma made the ham last as long as possible, over several meals, saving the bone to flavor beans and mush in the days to follow. They had been lucky in this. Not every slave was allowed to celebrate Christmas. Letty had discovered that on their travels as she spoke with others her age and shared experiences. How could someone grow up without Christmas?

"Christmas just another work day," her new-found friend Bet explained, "Worse. We baked and cooked for weeks for massa's Christmas. I glad when day over. Sometimes, if we good, the missus let us have left-overs from their table. Other times they fed left-overs to the pigs rather than share with us."

Letty shook her head in support. She knew what Bet was talking about.

Bet shrugged her shoulders. "No going back. No changing the past. I never believe in the white man's God. The missus, she made us go to church with her family on Christmas. I hated it. No, no Christmas for me. Jesus, he just the white man's God," she said.

Letty couldn't imagine. Was there a God for whites and another for blacks? What was her friend talking about? If that was so, she didn't want anything to do with a white God either. She had been taught there was only one God for everyone.

"Don't be lettin' that girl fill your head with nonsense," Sarai had told her later. "There only one God for black and white, but he black."

"Black?"

"That right. It a secret. We can't let white folk know. They think God their color. They wrong."

"How?"

"You seen pictures of people from those places where Jesus lived?"

"No."

"I have. The missus, she show me. She had a picture book of places from the Bible. The people, they black, so Jesus black. If God own son black, then God black."

"Sarai, what you going on about?" Ma asked.

"Nothin', just talkin' to Letty about Jesus, how he black."

"That kind of talk only lead to trouble," Ma said. "No more of it." Letty wondered about it later. She was too old to just accept what her ma said. She wanted to figure it out for herself.

When Letty asked Bet about God, her friend told her she didn't believe in God.

"Least not God in the Bible. I believe in God in trees and animals. My ma, she taught me spells and such. She taught me about herbs that heal people."

"She a witch?" Letty whispered.

"No, but she knew voodoo."

Letty didn't know what voodoo was, but she knew better than to ask her mother about it. She would never let Letty talk to Bet if she knew, and Letty wanted to talk to her. She wanted to know more about the practice. She wanted to learn which plants in the woods could be used for healing. She was sad when her friend moved on.

"We goin' further in Canada. Ma say it not safe here."

Such was life in Ontario. People were always moving through. Letty had thought that once they made it into Canada, they would be safe. But no, bounty hunters were waiting at night to catch unsuspecting runaway slaves as they crossed the Detroit River. The anti-slavery people had to be constantly vigilant and find new points of departure and landing spots lest they deliver their precious cargo into an ambush.

Ma and Sarai had joined with other members of their community to build a church, their own church. They included in the design a trap door and hiding place. If bounty hunters disturbed their services, there was a place to hide. They also built a tunnel to the Detroit River for slaves who had crossed and needed a hiding place. Letty had been proud to be part of the builders, contributing what she could from the meager earnings she made sewing and mending clothes.

Sarai was a seamstress. As such she had held a privileged position in her master's household. She spent many hours with her mistress and her children as she pinned and sewed clothes. Theirs had been a troubled relationship. Sarai's skin was pale, light enough to pass as white. Mulatto was the term. Letty knew about mulattos. No one talked about it, but she had overheard stories. How the master would have his choice of the women, even young girls. Letty knew her ma had wanted to spare her and her sister. When the master had started glancing their way, her ma had started talking with her daddy about leaving. Letty had heard them talk at night when they thought she was asleep.

Other girls had not escaped the unwanted attention of the plantation owners. They became large with child, giving birth to light-skinned babies. These babies were often hated by their mistresses as they were reminders of their husband's transgressions. This was the case for Sarai.

When Letty had met Sarai, Sarai was wearing a bonnet that hid the sides of her face. When she took it off at night and turned her face, Letty saw a large scar running across her cheek. She didn't dare ask Sarai about the scar.

When Sarai saw her staring at the scar, she explained. "The mistress, she no like me, no like the reminder of where I came from. She hate it when her husband slip away at night and stay in the overseer's cabin with different women, but she could do nothing to stop him. One mornin', after another such night, I came into her room with her coffee. She came at me, grabbed a hot poker from the fire and drew it across my face. 'You never be pretty enough to lure white men away from their home,' she said as she did it. Then she saw what she done and cried for help.

"'Help,' she yelled. When my ma came from the kitchen she said, 'She did it. She grabbed the poker, playin' with it and burned herself. I tried to stop her but it too late.' My ma, though, she know the truth. She look at the welt on my face. At first, I so surprised I didn't feel anythin'. Then it start to burn. It burned for forty days and forty nights. When it stopped burnin', I had this scar as a reminder to never trust white women." Sarai turned to let Letty see it better. "Go ahead and look. I not 'shamed. I wear the bonnet because it give me away to the bounty hunters, but here, alone at night, I don't have to hide. Let it be a reminder to you. It a blessin'. What man would want someone with a disfigured face? The massa never came near me. Beauty a curse for us women." Letty didn't want to look at the scar but found it hard to look away.

"Letty, stop starin'," her mother told her.

"It all right," Sarai assured her. "I got nothin' to hide." Sarai shifted on the ground, her face glowing in the flickering light of the fire.

"My mistress, she feel guilty after that. She try to make it up to me by keepin' me close, havin' me taught the skills of a seamstress. She not all bad. I feel sorry for her at times, so lonely on that big plantation, far away from her family. She told me about growing up on a plantation farther south. How her father doted on her. She thought her husband would dote on her too, but that didn't happen.

"She told me she missed her mother and father. I know what that like. One day, my mother sold and taken away. I begged my mistress to do somethin', but she said there nothin' she could do, it her husband's doin'. I know she had somethin' to do with it. She hated my mother but couldn't do anythin' to her as long as she my father's pet. When he moved to another slave, she made the arrangements." Sarai stared into the fire, as if watching it all again in the burning embers.

"I don't know that so, but I suspect that's how it happened. I vowed to leave when I could. But first I needed a trade so I focused on learnin'. I 'spect she kept me on more out of guilt over how she treated me and my mother, God-fearing Christian woman." Letty's mother, who had been sitting in the dark across from Sarai and Letty, grunted in agreement to that and nodded to encourage Sarai to continue.

"When I see my chance, I left."

"And we glad you did," Ma said. Over the course of their travel together, Sarai had shared more of her story. How she had passed as white to get passage on a boat across the Potomac.

Once they were settled in Canada, Sarai set about teaching Letty and her sister all she knew about sewing. Her mother took in laundry.

Between this and what Sarai and her sister made, they were able to get by.

"You need a trade," Sarai had said as they sewed under her watchful eye. "We can't count on a man to provide for us. Every woman should have the means to support herself." And so Letty had become a skilled seamstress.

Chapter 30

Detroit to Cascade Falls – Present Day

Letty locked the studio and headed for home over the Christmas holidays. She was ready to leave Detroit behind for a while.

She had held a small Christmas celebration for her students on the last day of classes, inviting her students from Sara's school to participate. It wasn't a recital, but it was fun. Some of the sparkle was missing because of the loss of the Pineda family. Letty hated coming into the empty building each day. Having a family living there had made the place feel less like an institution and more like a home. She missed Maryuri running into her arms to greet her and Alberto's smile and handshake — he was much too manly to give hugs any more. Without Rachel, Letty had thought she would have to cancel the fiesta and class of Honduran traditional dance, but others from the neighborhood, friends of Rachel's, had come forward to help her organize the party. It was a Christmas fiesta with traditional Honduran dances, other dances of the Caribbean and Central America.

"It is what Rachel would have wanted," her friends told Letty.

Thanks to Sara's suggestion that she invite children from the neighborhood to attend classes for free, she had a passable number of students but had yet to make any money on the dance studio. The money she took in for tuition went back into the studio to pay for advertising and printing costs. She had not added any classes. She wouldn't have been able to pay the instructors. And so she had been relegated to teaching every class she offered, mostly for young children. She loved the children, but missed more challenging dance routines. She tried to make up for this through her own practice. She did not want to lose any ability. She felt her foot growing stronger with each day, possibly stronger than before the break. The possibility of maybe going back to Alvin Ailey remained in the outskirts of her mind as an escape hatch. If this didn't work, she could always go back, couldn't she? But not if she let herself get flabby.

With so little income coming in, Letty didn't think she would ever be able to move out of Sara's apartment. She appreciated the gift of space but since that board meeting, things just weren't the same between her and Sara. They still worked together. Sara still helped out, but their relationship had changed. Perhaps Sara had been right. If so, Letty wasn't ready to admit it.

She was ready to go home and crash for a while. She luxuriated in her old bed the first morning back, so comfortable with all of her belongings, familiar scents and sounds. She could smell coffee coming up from downstairs, beckoning to her to come down. And was that her mama's French toast? But her covers beckoned too. She listened to the voices of her parents talking in the kitchen just like they had every morning of her life.

Finally her mother called up to her. "Leticia, breakfast is on the table." Letty crawled out of the comfort of her bed, threw on a bathrobe and went downstairs.

"It smells so good, Mom. Heavenly."

"We were beginning to think you would sleep all day if we let you."

"I would have." Letty sat down in front of the cup of coffee that was setting at her place.

"You'll have plenty of time to sleep while you are here. You don't have to do it all in one day," her dad said. Her mother gave her a slice of French toast.

"Sausage?" her mother asked.

"No, Mom. I've got to stay in shape."

"For what?"

"For if I ever want to dance professionally again."

"I thought that was behind you," her mother said.

"Let the girl be, Alicia," her dad intervened. "She just got home. You have all vacation to interrogate her, when I'm not around."

"Then don't you have to get to work," her mom said as her dad stood up, cleared his plate from the table and excused himself.

Letty's mom sat down kitty-corner from her, coffee mug in hand. "Now it's just us. Tell me what's going on."

"Nothing, Mom."

"I know when something is wrong with my baby. Tell me."

"Well," Letty sighed. "I'm just not sure I did the right thing, quitting Alvin Ailey, moving to Detroit."

"Why do you say that?"

"Because, I don't seem to be getting anywhere."

"Where did you expect to be by now?" her mother raised her coffee cup to her lips and stared at her over the steaming mug.

"I don't know. Just further along than I am. I'm just getting by financially, and that's with a free apartment. And then there was the situation with the Pinedas."

"I know. That was terrible, but, you know, it happens all the time."

"I know. I know. And there's problems with the board."

"Sounds pretty normal to me. What are the problems?" Her mother continued to sip her coffee while Letty responded.

"I just, I thought I would get more support from them. I thought that we were in this together."

"And your board probably figures they brought you in so they wouldn't have to do so much."

"Whose side are you on?"

"I'm not on anyone's side. I'm just saying, that's life with a board." She set her coffee cup on the table. "It's normal to have differing expectations. Happens all the time, especially with new boards. There are diverse boards that function differently. Some boards are more hands-on. The members are actively involved in the ministry of the organization, but those are usually smaller organizations, not big enough to have paid staff."

"I'm not exactly paid."

"I thought they had started paying you."

"Haven't got the money yet. I have to raise the money for my salary."

"That has to change." Her mother shook her head and raised her mug again.

"It's okay. What I'm more upset about is that they didn't support me when I wanted to open a legal services clinic."

"You what? You wanted to open a legal services clinic? Baby girl, what were you thinking?" The mug came down.

"I was thinking, there's a lot of people in need of legal help who can't afford it. People like the Pinedas. How hard could it be to get a group of lawyers together, have them volunteer their time?"

"Leticia, your board did you a favor. They were acting responsibly. A legal clinic is a good idea, but do you have any idea how much work it would take to get it up and running?"

"Apparently I don't. That's all people keep telling me."

"Then maybe it's time you listened. It's hard work and would divert you from your original mission to support the arts."

"Okay, okay. I get it. I was wrong."

"Your board acted responsibly by not authorizing you to go down that route."

"I get it, Mom. Can we move on to something else?"

"Baby girl, I just want what's best for you."

"I know mom, and I appreciate that."

Letty and her mom sat in silence for a few minutes, each sipping their coffee.

"So, tell me. How are things between you and Walter? His parents told me you were dating." Her mom looked over the rim of her cup.

"Really, Mom. We aren't dating."

"Between you and Jerome, I'll never have grandbabies."

Letty picked at her French toast.

"Thank you for visiting your Aunt Letty," her mother started again. "It's so hard to get away to see her. I'm sure she appreciates it. And if she doesn't, I do."

"It's not so bad, visiting her. I like it most of the time."

"Has she told you much of the family history?"

"On her better days. I wish I knew more."

"You know your great, great, great …"

"— I know, five times great."

"… grandparents were among the first middle class black families in Cascade Falls. They had their own businesses, owned their home."

"Yes, Grandpa's barbershop. The one Uncle Nick still owns."

"That's right. They worked hard so their children could have a better future. It's all any parent wants for their children. Freedom. The freedom to choose what path they want to take. Freedom to live the life they want. Freedom to pursue happiness. That's all I want for you, baby. I want you to be happy."

"I want that too, Mom. I'm just not sure what that is, what route I need to take."

"And move back to Cascade Falls and give me grandchildren." Letty laughed at her mom's words. Her mom stood up. "I guess I better be going as well. I'll see you later, for dinner," she said as she left, leaving Letty sitting at the table.

What to do with the day? She could crawl back into bed, but once out, bed didn't seem so inviting. She decided to pack her dance clothes and go to Joy's School of Dance. Chloe had given her a key so she would be able to keep up her practice.

Letty drove through the lightly snow-covered roads to downtown Cascade Falls, parked and put the key in the lock. It was a familiar routine. One she had done for years when she had worked at the school of dance. Memories flooded her brain as she walked through the doors. There, before her, was the realization of years of work. The first floor held office space. When she had left only a few of the offices had been filled. Now it looked like each office space was filled with a different non-profit or business devoted to health and healing. Joy's legacy. The large old building now was a bustling center for the arts and healing. Classes were still being offered by the small ceramic shop. The small gift shop they had started years ago with cards, books on healing, ballet and other dance gear, now held a prominent space on the first floor. There was a naturopath, offering natural oils and health food, a massage therapist and a yoga store. All were closed for the Christmas holidays.

Letty rode the elevator to the third floor. She was hit with another wave of memory and nostalgia when she stepped out into the dance school. The picture of Joy, pregnant with Grace, still held a prominent position on the wall. She stopped before the picture before proceeding to the changing room. She unlocked the door to the main classroom, turned on the large space heater to warm up the room without heating the whole top floor and walked about the room, gently touching the bar and looking at herself in the floor length mirror. She wore warm leggings over top of her tights and a loose-fitting long sweater to keep herself warm till she was warmed-up. Her hair was pulled up into a bun with a heavy head band covering her ears and warming her head.

She remembered a little girl, attending her first dance class, over twenty years ago. Joy had made it fun. She had come back year after year. In high school she spent more time here than home, if you didn't count time sleeping. Joy had encouraged her in her dancing, arranging for her to try out for Juilliard her senior year and supporting her when she didn't get in. Joy would have been proud of her getting into Alvin Ailey.

Letty started her routine, stretching to warm up her muscles, bending over her outstretched legs then standing at the bar, raising her leg to her head. When she was ready, she pulled out her iPod and started music for her work-out routine. She started slow then built up speed as she went from traditional ballet to the more fluid movements of lyrical dance then back again. Years of practice converged into one dance routine as Letty lost herself in the movement, forgetting everything but this moment. One minute she was running, running for her life, running away. Then she was running to something. She didn't know what she was running to or what she was running from. She whirled on her bare toes then slowed to a stop. As the music ended, she heard a thin stream of applause echo throughout the empty room.

"Nicely done."

Letty turned around and saw Sara standing in the doorway.

"How did you get in here?" Letty asked.

"I suspect the same way you did. Keys." Sara held up the keys she had gotten from Chloe.

"I mean, what are you doing here?"

"I brought some artwork for the gallery."

"New pieces?"

"Yes. You should check them out when you are done up here."

"I will." Letty did a few more dances and a cool-down before leaving. The practice room was her sanctuary, dance her prayer. She felt Joy's presence all around her.

Letty changed her clothes and walked down the stairs to the art gallery on the second floor. She found Sara hanging pictures. She had a couple new charcoal sketches she was displaying. Most of the pictures in the gallery were for sale, with ten percent of the sale price going to support Joy's Center for the Arts. Sara didn't make many sales, still every bit helped out, as Letty knew from her years running the dance studio.

"What do you think?" Sara asked as Letty approached her. Sara had done a series of sketches featuring Rachel and her children, one showing them being taken out by the immigration agents.

"I'm working on an oil painting on the situation of immigrants in our country. I'm using Rachel, how I remember her, as the model for that. I have two different backgrounds, one in Honduras, one here, working in the fields. I'm not completely sure how it is going to end up. That one I plan to hang in our gallery at Freedom House."

"You did all of these since that last board meeting?"

"I guess I needed the right inspiration. Seeing Rachel and her children being taken away by ICE, that did it." Sara hung the last sketch, putting them in places where other sketches that had not sold had hung. "I like to rotate pictures so visitors see different work each time they come. Gives them a reason to come back and see what's new," Sara explained.

"You know, Letty," Sara put the pictures she had removed into a carry case then turned towards Letty. "What I said after that board meeting, about you losing sight of what you were meant to do. I think that I was saying that more to me than you. I mean, I had lost sight of why I had gotten involved in the first place. I had lost sight of what was most important to me. I think I was scared."

"Scared of what?"

"Scared that I didn't have what it takes to be an artist. That I'd never make it. That I'd spend hours on paintings and charcoal drawings that just clutter my studio. That no one will ever see, much less buy my art. That I'm taking time away from my family, my kids, my husband, and for what?"

"But you have gotten positive feedback on your work. You sold that one picture at the auction a few years ago. And that doctor, Julia Hennessey. Wasn't her father going to introduce you to some famous artist?"

"He was, did. And he has been great. He has given me some great feedback on my art. Said he would help me when I was ready for a show in New York."

"So, what's the hold up? How long ago was that? What are you waiting for?"

"It's easier said than done. To do a show in New York, I not only need a patron ..."

"—which you have."

"... I need a body of work that is sufficiently ready."

"You don't have that?"

"Not yet. Not that I feel confident about. First it was the kids. I said I couldn't give it the time I needed because of the twins. And then, I got involved in setting up Freedom House. And then you came along."

"I'm sorry, Sara."

"No, that's not what I mean at all. They were all excuses. Convenient excuses to not have to face that blank canvas and wonder how I was going to fill it. Excuses so I didn't have to risk failure. I could say, if only I had the time, I could have been great, instead of facing the reality that maybe I'm just not that good."

"You'll never know unless you give it your best."

"I guess. Sometimes I think I'd rather not know."

"I hear you." Letty shook her head in agreement.

"What about you?" Sara asked.

"I had my shot."

"What do you mean?"

"I mean, I had my shot. I danced with Alvin Ailey. I was good enough to do that. That's as far as I'll go as a dancer." It hurt to hear what she had been telling herself for months. Hearing it was different from keeping the thought in the deep recesses of her mind.

"Wow, twenty-seven and already a has-been." Letty smiled at Sara's response.

"Sort of. I could have kept dancing for years. I was good enough. But I wasn't one of the 'greats.' I'm not another Misty Copeland or Baryshnikov, and that's okay. I'm the best version of me that I can be."

"What do you do next?"

"Next? I'm not done yet. Some would say I'm just beginning. I've got a good role model in Joy. Just think of all the young lives she touched over the years." If she told herself that enough, would she finally believe it?

"Don't I know."

"And I've got a good friend who has only just begun to realize her ability as an artist."

Sara laughed. "I can see where reminding her about that could be a full-time job."

"Don't even." They both laughed. "But really, Sara, I do still have some connections in New York when you're ready for that show."

"I just have to get my act together. Besides, I think when I'm ready to do that big show, I'd like to do it in Detroit."

"Really? I happen to have some connections there too. Have you heard of Freedom House? Let's chat over lunch. I see a great future for you." They laughed as they walked out of the building, Sara carrying the pictures she was taking back with her, Letty carrying her dance bag.

Chapter 31

Cascade Falls – Present Day

Dale sat in darkness with his family, lit only by the candles they were holding until the opening procession and placement of the baby Jesus in the manger. Ava sat next to him on one side, Jacob and Grace next to Ava. Ashley sat next to him on the other side. For a moment Dale thought maybe something had changed with her. The service was beautiful with candles lighting the darkness, children acting out the first Christmas, Christmas carols. How could she not be affected?

Joe's message had spoken directly to his heart when he spoke of a wayward daughter that seemed to have gone astray and gotten with child. That girl of Ashley's age had been the bearer of the Christ child. How Mary's parents had probably wondered where they had gone wrong, not just in their daughter being pregnant, but then claiming that God was the father, that the child to be was the long-awaited Savior. How crazy was that?

Joe wondered out loud in his sermon how many other pregnant teens had made the same claim back then. We don't hear about them in the Bible but there are many equally crazy claims made by people today, people with mental problems in institutions. How many "Jesuses" were there in the local psych ward? Joe had told him about them, people who claimed to be God. Only Mary had been the real deal. How had her parents dealt with it? The Bible doesn't give any clues. It only talked about Joseph and his concern not to embarrass his fiancé. Had Mary's parents believed her? Had they stuck by her?

Ashley, though, was no Mary. Far from it. He didn't understand her, any more than Mary's parents had understood Mary, but he would try to stick by her. He would see her through this to the other side, no matter how long it took, he promised himself.

Dale looked across the crowded church to where his sister Kathleen sat with her two sons and Joe's two daughters. Stephanie was round with child, just how Mary must have looked over two thousand years ago. Was Joe preaching to himself? Or to Stephanie? Or to any number of the parents in the congregation who struggled to understand their children? Or was God speaking to him, through this fallible man? A man he knew far too well now after all they had been through together, all they knew about each other? Yet God could still speak to him through this man.

He reached for Ava's hand and gave it a squeeze as the choir led the congregation in singing, "Hark the Herald, Angels Sing." Whether Ashley was getting anything or not out of the service, he knew that he could get through this just as he had gotten through other crises. They would get through this together.

Chapter 32

Cascade Falls – Present Day

Letty wasn't surprised to see Walter at church for the Christmas Eve candlelight service. He was attending with his parents just as she was attending with her parents. Her brother Jerome was going to meet them after the service for snacks and gifts, as was their custom. At one point, Jerome had bowed out of attending church services.

"Just not for me, sis," he had told her. Their mother had it out with him at first, then reluctantly accepted the situation.

"Alicia, we raised our children to think for themselves, then get angry when they do just that and don't do what we want them to do. What do you expect?" Letty remembered her dad saying.

"I expect my babies to set their butts in the pew," her mom had responded.

"He will, when he's ready. When he has the right situation, the right reason."

Letty was surprised when Jerome showed up at the service, sliding into the pew with a young woman. Her dad looked over at her mom and smiled. "The right situation," she heard him say.

After church, Walter sought her out and stopped her.

"Do you mind if I borrow your daughter for a moment?" he asked her parents.

"Keep her as long as you want," her dad joked.

"Not funny, Dad," Letty said.

"You're welcome to come over for some food," her mother told him.

"Thank you for the invite, but my parents are expecting me."

"Your parents are welcome too."

Walter pulled Letty aside. "I don't know what I did or didn't do that you are so angry with me."

"I'm not angry at you."

"Then why have you been avoiding me?"

"I'm more angry at myself."

"About what?"

"Too complicated to explain now." Letty looked over at her parents. Walter's parents were talking to them.

"Would you give me a chance? I'm willing to listen."

"Maybe. After the holidays are over."

"I was hoping we could do it before the holidays are over, hoping you would be my date for New Year's Eve. I hate to stay home and hate even more to go out alone."

"What about Marjorie?"

"I told you. She's a colleague. We work together. That's all."

"I'll think about it."

"Then you'll answer my calls?"

"Okay. That's only fair. I'll answer your calls."

Walter reached into his inner pocket and pulled out an envelope. "Oh, and I have a gift for you." He handed her the envelope.

"I don't have anything for you." Letty accepted the envelope, unsure whether to give it back to him unopened.

"It's not a big deal. Open it," Walter insisted.

Letty opened the envelope and pulled out what appeared to be two green cards. "What's this?" She held up the cards and looked at Walter.

"Copies of green cards for Rachel and Carlos."

"You mean?" Letty shook her head. "How did you? I thought it wasn't possible."

"I called in some favors. I know how upset you were about that whole situation. I got them jobs with a hotel that's part of a chain owned by one of our clients. They always need workers. I put in a good word for them. Carlos is doing maintenance and grounds keeping. Rachel is working in the kitchen. It's not much. The pay isn't the greatest, but at least now they won't be deported."

Letty looked at him, her eyes wide. "You did this for me?"

"And for myself. I'm not heartless, Letty. I do care about the downtrodden. It's part of my swearing in as a lawyer. Can't a person be a corporate lawyer and still have a heart?"

"I guess they can. How can I thank you?"

"Go out with me on New Year's Eve."

"Okay. I will."

Walter started to lean in for a kiss, then thought better of it as they saw both sets of parents watching them. Instead he hugged her.

"Merry Christmas," Walter said.

"Merry Christmas," Letty said as she pulled back. "And thank you." She held up the envelope. "This is the best present you could have given me."

Chapter 33

Cascade Falls – Present Day

Kathleen glanced at Stephanie as Joe preached about Mary, the wayward daughter. Was he getting a little too close for comfort? One of the perils of living with a preacher is that their family life can be easy fodder for preaching. Stephanie and Michelle had grown up with it. Kathleen was just beginning to experience what it was like. Not that Joe blatantly shared family secrets in his sermons, yet there was always the danger of church members reading into what he said, or worse. A kernel of truth used as part of a sermon could feel like a gross violation of privacy. It was no secret that Stephanie was pregnant. There she was in all her pregnant glory. How could people not read into what Joe was saying? She wondered what Stephanie was thinking. If she was listening, she showed no sign of hearing.

Stephanie wasted no time in letting her dad know what she thought about his sermon.

"So, Dad," she said on the ride home. "Real subtle."

"What are you talking about?"

"Your sermon about the wayward daughter. Like, was there anyone in church who didn't get the point?"

"I was talking about Mary and her situation with her parents. It was for any parent who struggles to understand their children, not just about you. Not everything is about you."

"And it just so happens, you have an out-of-control, pregnant daughter," Stephanie said.

"It wasn't directed at you," Joe defended himself.

"I'm with Stephanie on this, Dad," Michelle stated. "Major embarrassing."

Kathleen reached over and placed her hand on Joe's thigh and gave him a reassuring squeeze.

Josh, Scott and Alex, Scott's girlfriend, met them at home. Stephanie was out of the car the minute it stopped and rushed into the house.

"What's up with her?" Scott asked.

"Dad's sermon," Michelle said.

"What about it?" Josh asked.

"He talked about wayward pregnant daughters," Michelle explained.

"Oh, that. I guess I didn't listen. No offense, Pastor Joe. I don't listen to anyone's sermons, not just yours," Josh said. "I'll talk to her."

Josh sought out Stephanie while Kathleen went to the kitchen and got out the trays of food she and her mom had prepared earlier that day. Sliced ham, roast beef, and turkey for bread or rolls. Cheese slices, cubes and crackers. A relish tray with pickles, olives, artichokes and spiced and pickled veggies. Shrimp and cocktail sauce. And Christmas cookies, lots of them.

"Just because it's Christmas doesn't mean you can eat everything in sight," Esther said on the drive over to Kathleen and Joe's. Peter kept his eyes on the road in front of him.

"Okay. I'll refrain from eating the furniture,"

"You know what I mean." Peter had been given a reprieve by his doctor. Six months after his heart attack, his doctor gave him the go ahead to add some butter and cheese to his diet.

"This doesn't mean you can go 'hog-wild'," his doctor had joked, knowing Peter's penchant for all things porcine, especially processed meats, ham, sausage, hot dogs and sausages.

"It also doesn't mean you can go back to adding cheese to everything you eat and cooking in butter, pouring butter on your popcorn and potatoes," Esther had told him on the drive home from his doctor appointment.

Peter hadn't responded to that comment at the time.

"Did you hear me? Or do you just not want to answer?" she had asked.

"I heard you. Let me bask in the permission to add cheese and butter to my diet for a while, would you?"

"Fair enough," Esther had agreed. He figured there'd be time enough to argue about what "some" meant later.

She lectured him about watching his portions on the drive over. All on deaf ears. Esther's definition of "some" was significantly different from his.

He didn't respond now to the latest comment. Yes, he knew what she meant. How could he not?

"Did you hear me?" Esther asked.

"Do we spend the rest of our life arguing about what I can and can't eat, or do we just enjoy the time we have together?"

"Can't we do both?"

"Not if you are going to give me that 'look' every time I eat a piece of cheese or butter a roll."

"I don't give you a look."

"You most certainly do. What else would you call it?"

"A caring gesture of concern."

Peter laughed. "Okay. How can I enjoy my food if you are always giving me caring gestures of concern?"

"That's the point, I want you to think before you pile on the butter and cheese."

"Or maybe you can trust me to know what I'm doing …"

"—not where cheese and butter are concerned."

"… and let me enjoy my food."

"I hope you enjoy it in the hospital because that's where your diet is going to land you."

"Esther, like I said, we can continue this argument for the rest of our lives, or enjoy the time we have together. I don't know about you, but I'd rather be able to enjoy my life, even if I die sooner, than live to be one hundred eating twigs and berries. What good is a life half lived?"

"Ditto!" came from the back seat where Grandpop, Esther's dad, sat quietly. "Did you forget I was here? I'm with Peter on this."

"But it would be one hundred years with me, Dad. Isn't that worth taking care of yourself? I thought that was the plan, to grow old together," Esther diverted her attention back to Peter.

"That still is the plan," Peter said. "I'm not planning on leaving any time soon, but I don't want to live my life in a way that makes me want to leave it. I plan to enjoy my life."

"And I plan to do that too," Esther said as Peter pulled into the driveway of what used to be their home. "We'll talk about this later," Esther said as they helped Grandpop out of the car.

"That we will, I'm sure," Peter said. He knew he would hear about it sooner, rather than later.

"Kids, make way for your grandpop," Kathleen admonished her kids as her mom came in with Peter and Grandpop. She took her grandfather's coat while Joe took her mom and Peter's coats and hung them up for them.

"I'm not an invalid," her mom told Kathleen as she walked into the kitchen to help, leaning on her cane.

"I know, Mom, but everything is already on the table. I want you to just enjoy Christmas. You've certainly done your part over the years."

"I enjoy helping out."

"Okay. You can take out the napkins and silverware."

Esther carried in the basket that contained the napkins and plastic silverware and placed it at the front of the table, next to the paper plates.

"Time to eat," she proclaimed when Kathleen came in. "Help yourself everyone." Not that anyone needed instructions for the traditional Christmas Eve buffet.

Kathleen saw her mom watch as Peter filled his plate with meat and cheeses and slathered butter on a roll. He certainly was taking advantage of his new-found freedom to add cheese and butter to his diet.

"Where's Stephanie?" Peter asked as everyone filled their plates. Kathleen recognized the diversion tactic to take her mom's attention away from him. She doubted it would work.

"In her room. She's a little under the weather," Kathleen said.

"She's sulking," Michelle said.

"Didn't like her dad's sermon?" Peter suggested.

"And that," Michelle added.

"It was for all parents. Something most parents could relate too," Kathleen defended her husband.

"I could relate," her mom said, looking at Kathleen. "I know something about wayward daughters. It's hard sometimes to let your kids make their own mistakes, find their own way."

"And husbands, too," Peter added. Kathleen saw the look her mom shot Peter.

"Look how good I turned out," Kathleen said in her own defense.

"That you did," her mom agreed. "Your kids are going to go their own way, whether we like it or not. Still, I imagine it was a little awkward for Stephanie, her being pregnant and all."

"You think? Try majorly awkward. It was awkward for me, being her sister," Michelle said.

"And to think, I used to want to know what people said about my sermons after church was over," Joe said.

"Don't worry, Joe. Like Josh said earlier. Most people don't listen, and if they do listen, they forget by the time they get home," Scott said.

"Why doesn't that make me feel any better?" Joe said. "Let's not say any more about this when Stephanie comes downstairs."

"Say what?" Stephanie asked as she walked into the dining room followed by Josh.

"Nothing, dear," Joe said. "Can I get you a plate?"

"I'm pregnant, Dad. Not helpless." Stephanie picked up a paper plate, looked across the table, then bent over in a cramp.

"You okay, Stephanie?" Kathleen asked, putting her arm around Stephanie's waist and holding her up.

"Just a killer cramp," Stephanie said as she took a deep breath.

"Or labor pain," Kathleen suggested.

"Is this how it's supposed to feel?" Stephanie asked.

"Like the worse cramps ever? Like your body is getting ready to split apart?"

"Yeah."

"Sounds pretty normal to me. How long in between pains?" Kathleen asked.

"I don't know. I've had some pain off and on all day. This was the worst one."

"Could be Braxton-Hicks," Kathleen's mother suggested.

"What's that?"

"False labor pains before the real ones begin," her mom explained.

"If that was a false one, I'd hate to imagine what a real one is like."

"Why don't you sit down for a while and see if the pains come back." Kathleen led her out of the dining room and sat her in a comfortable, soft chair.

"I won't be able to get up out of this chair," she said.

"That's okay. There are enough people here to help you. Just relax." Kathleen sat next to Stephanie on a straight back chair.

Josh came in with a plate with a few shrimp and some cheese and crackers for her. "Here, Stephanie, I brought you some food."

"Thank you, Josh. But I don't feel like eating."

"You have to keep up your strength," Josh insisted, setting the plate in what remained of Stephanie's lap.

"That's okay, Josh. Stephanie will eat when she's ready to eat. Give her a few minutes."

Kathleen went back into the dining room, finished putting food on her plate, came back and sat back down next to Stephanie.

"You sure you're all right?" she leaned over and asked.

"I wish people would stop asking me that," Stephanie replied.

"A baby on Christmas. Now that would be a gift," Grandpop said.

"That's okay, Grandpop. A baby any day is a gift," Kathleen said. "The baby will be born when the baby is good and ready to be born."

"Could we please talk about something else?" Stephanie asked.

"Sure, Stephanie," Scott said. "Uncle Dale and Aunt Ava and the kids coming over?"

"Not this year. They're going to their other grandparents for Christmas Eve. Then we'll have Christmas dinner at their home."

"Oh, right. I forgot where they were in the rotation," Scott said.

"I hope we'll get a chance to see Sara, Larry and the twins tomorrow," Peter said.

"I think so. They are in town staying with Sara's parents. I don't know if they are going to Larry's parents tomorrow or not." The chit-chat went back and forth over insignificant details, trivial matters that make up life.

"Seems funny, not having any children around at Christmas," her mom said.

"That's why we have Michelle here," Josh teased his step-sister. "You're the baby."

Michelle prepared to retort when Stephanie doubled over in pain, dropping her plate of food onto the floor. She struggled to get up. Kathleen put her plate down and helped her get up.

"What's going on?" Stephanie asked through the pain

"I believe you are in labor," Kathleen said. "Maybe we'll have that Christmas baby after all." She put her arms around her stepdaughter. "I think it's time we get you to the hospital. Josh, get her bag from her bedroom. Joe, get the car started. I'll help Stephanie out." Scott got Stephanie's coat out of the closet and helped her into it while Kathleen continued to support her.

"Breathe, Stephanie. Just breathe," Kathleen told her.

"Does this mean?" Stephanie asked.

"Yes, it means you're going to have your baby. Mom, call the hospital. They'll call Stephanie's doctor."

"But Stephanie's doctor is in Kalamazoo," Josh said as he came into the room carrying Stephanie's overnight bag.

"Then they'll alert the ob-gyn on call."

"Here, Mom. I'll help Stephanie." Josh took over from Kathleen, wrapping his arm around her shoulders to support her. "After all, I'm her Lamaze coach."

"Okay." Kathleen didn't fight him on this. Josh climbed into the back seat of the car with Stephanie. Kathleen climbed into the front.

"What about us?" Scott rapped on the window until Joe rolled it down.

"Go back in and finish up. You keep Grandma, Peter and Grandpop company." Kathleen yelled over Joe to him.

"No way I'm missing this," Kathleen heard Scott say as Joe rolled the window back up.

Chapter 34

Joe drove out of the driveway and rushed to the hospital. Stephanie was wheeled into the emergency room, taken up to obstetrics and given a room.

"Are you the father?" the nurse asked Josh.

"No, the brother. But I'm her Lamaze coach."

"Okay. You stay. The rest of you, out."

"Here we go again," Kathleen said to Joe after they were chased out of Stephanie's room to the empty waiting room. "Once again at the hospital." Joe got Kathleen a cup of coffee from a pot that had clearly been sitting for too long.

"Ugh," Kathleen grimaced as she took a sip.

"Sorry. That's all they have. They have vending machine coffee on the second floor. I can get you some."

"No. That would be worse. I'll do without."

Scott, Alex and Michelle joined them.

"What about Grandma, Peter and Grandpop?" Kathleen asked.

"They went home. Said they'd had enough excitement for one night. We put the food away and came over. No way I'm going to miss out on this. I'm going to be an uncle," Scott said.

"And I'm going to be an aunt," Michelle added.

"And I'm with him," Alex said, holding onto Scott's arm.

"Too bad you didn't bring any food with you," Joe said.

"I snuck some Christmas cookies in my pockets," Michelle said as she pulled out four cookies. "Almost enough for everyone."

"We'll make do," Joe said.

"Since you didn't bring enough for everyone, you're the one who has to miss out," Scott told her.

"Hey, no fair," Michelle said.

"Sure it is. That's the rule. Right, Mom? Like whoever cuts the pie takes the last piece to make sure they cut enough for everyone."

"I think this is different, Scott. Michelle was nice enough to offer to share. I'll go without," Kathleen told him.

"Suit yourself, Mom." Scott grabbed the biggest cookie and took a bite. "How long do you think we'll be here?"

"It takes as long as it takes," Joe said

"Anybody bring any cards?" Scott asked.

"Didn't think about it," Joe said. "Sorry."

"We could sing Christmas carols," Michelle suggested.

"Yeah, and wait for Santa," Scott said.

"Just a suggestion," Michelle said.

Alex poked Scott in the ribs. "I think it's a great idea," she said. "Who's ready?" They broke into a feeble chorus of Silent Night then tried Rudolph the Red-Nosed Reindeer.

"Come on, who doesn't think this is lame?" Scott asked.

"We are pretty pathetic," Michelle agreed.

"How long have we been here?" Scott looked at his watch. "Half an hour. Is that all? Are there any snacks here?"

Kathleen looked at Joe, remembering a similar evening, waiting for Sara's babies, when they had gone downstairs for snacks.

"There's the vending machines downstairs," Kathleen said.

"We'll go." Scott got up and pointed to Alex.

"No, that's okay. Joe and I will go. Right, honey?" Kathleen stood up as the doors to the waiting room opened followed by a chorus of "We Wish You a Merry Christmas."

"Ho, ho, ho," Julia, Alex's mom, and Henry, Julia's husband, came in bearing gifts.

"I hear there's a party here," Julia said. She handed Kathleen a coffee. "Do you have any idea how hard it is to find a coffee shop open on Christmas Eve? Lucky for you, the local Speedway has good coffee."

"I hope those bags contain something to eat," Scott eyed the packages.

"Alex texted me what was happening. Told me to bring food and cards. So here we are." Julia pulled snack mix, chips and dips, tortilla chips and guacamole, and Christmas cookies out of the boxes.

"Who's up for a game of euchre?" Henry pulled two decks of cards out of his pockets.

By midnight, only the kids were still playing cards, while Joe and Kathleen and Julia and Henry leaned against each other, in and out of sleep. By one o'clock, Joe and Henry were snoring, and by two o'clock, even the youngsters had given up. Alex and Scott sat next to each, holding each other up. Michelle stretched out on a couch. Kathleen slept fitfully, waking every hour or so and checking the time. Around four o'clock, she was awakened by the sound of a lullaby, coming over the hospital PA system.

"What was that? It sounded like harp music, angel harps," Michelle sat up and yawned.

"What did you hear?" Julia asked.

"Sounded like a lullaby," Kathleen said.

"That's what the hospital plays whenever a baby is born. Since there's no one else here waiting, Stephanie must have had her baby." Julia sat up and jabbed Henry awake.

Kathleen poked Joe in the ribs, "Wake up. We think the baby is here."

"Really," Joe said as he shook his head awake. "Is it a boy or a girl?"

"We don't know yet."

"Then how do you know the baby is here?"

"Because we heard the harp music."

"Yeah, Dad. It was like angel music," Michelle said.

A nurse came into the waiting room. "Michaels' family?" she asked. When Joe nodded, she added, "You have a baby boy."

"A boy," Joe repeated after the nurse.

"Yes, Grandpa, a boy," Kathleen said and kissed him.

"Grandma." Joe kissed her back. Grandma, for all of her preparation, Kathleen wasn't sure she liked the sound of that.

Chapter 35

Cascade Falls – Present Day

Letty was surprised when Chloe asked her if she had time for some one-on-one training with Ashley.

"How did Ashley know I would be around?" Letty asked.

"You know Ashley. She has her way. She's pretty determined," Chloe told her.

"Determined about what?"

"To be a dancer. She's significantly improved since you last saw her dance. Maybe she wants to show you how much." Letty wondered about that. If she knew Ashley, she had something else in mind. Still she agreed to meet Chloe and Ashley at the dance studio the day after Christmas.

Letty warmed up with Ashley then had her perform a routine for her.

"Anything in particular?" Ashley asked.

"That depends. What are you most interested in? What are your goals?"

"Ballet. I plan to study at Juilliard then dance with the American Ballet Company with Misty Copeland."

"That's pretty specific," Letty commented.

"Did you meet Misty Copeland when you were in New York?" Ashley asked.

"No, but I did see her dance on several occasions. She is quite gifted."

"That's what I plan to do." No lack of confidence here, Letty thought.

"Ashley," Chloe joined the conversation. "Do the routine you put together for the Christmas recital. Ashley had a solo," she explained to Letty. She turned on the music for the routine when Ashley nodded her readiness. Watching the girl, Letty was impressed. She definitely had talent, more natural talent than Letty had.

"Well done, Ashley. I can see improvement since you last danced for me," Letty told her.

"Then you'll teach me?"

"Wait. What are you talking about? You know I live in Detroit."

"I can live with my aunt Sara while you teach me."

"Teach you?"

"Yes, get me ready for Juilliard. Help me with the audition."

"I don't know, Ashley. I'm not sure I'm the best person to do this. I haven't focused solely on ballet but have worked at learning and integrating other dance styles."

"You're the best around here."

Letty looked over at Chloe. "Did you know about this?" she asked her friend.

"No, this is the first I've heard about this. She is right, though. You are the best dancer to come through the school. My training has been even more eclectic than yours. And when I was dancing in New York it was in musicals, not classical ballet."

Letty looked back at Ashley. From what Chloe had told her, Ashley had become much more focused and disciplined this year, but would that be enough? Even more important, was she the right teacher for her? Did she have what it would take to prepare Ashley for the rigor of Juilliard and professional dance?

"What about your parents? What do they say about this?"

"They don't know yet. But if you and Aunt Sara talk to them …"

Letty shook her head as she took it all in. What was the right thing to do?

"Besides," Ashley continued to push her point. "They are so passé. They insist I go to church with them every Sunday even though I've outgrown that."

"Wait, Ashley. If this is just an end-run around your parents … I won't be any part of it."

"No, it's not. Church is a secondary issue. I really want to attend Juilliard. The acceptance rate is only six percent. The best way for me to get in is to have the right teacher. Will you do it?"

"What about school?"

"I can finish up high school online, or not. I can get a GED if I have to. Juilliard accepts GEDs."

"What about money? Are your parents able to afford Juilliard? And how will you afford living in Detroit?"

"I can live with Aunt Sara for free and help you with classes at your dance studio."

"We can't afford to pay you, at least not right away."

"You can pay me with dance instructions. Please Letty. I just have to get out of Cascade Falls. If I don't leave here, I'll never reach my goals."

"Sounds like you've done your research." Letty looked at Chloe. "What do you think?"

"Juilliard is extremely difficult to get in. I can't give Ashley the training she needs to make it."

Letty sighed. She remembered her audition for Juilliard, how disappointed she had been when she didn't get in. How Joy, Ashley's mother, had encouraged her not to give up. Perhaps if she had received more personal attention and training? But no, Joy had done her best to prepare her. She just wasn't as talented as Ashley. What would Joy say? Would she be okay with her daughter moving away from home to Detroit to study dance?

"Okay. But there are a number of conditions. First, your parents have to be okay with this, and your aunt Sara has to agree as well. You have to keep up your studies. I know Juilliard will accept a GED in place of high school graduation, but I won't and I doubt your parents would agree to that. You won't be able to attend Juilliard if you don't graduate from high school. And, you need to be serious about this. If I ever see you not taking this as seriously as you need to, I'll send you back home."

"Thank you, Letty," Ashley hugged her. "You won't regret it."

"But will you? Are you sure you want to do this? Miss out on high school, prom, dances, senior activities, all the fun of high school?" Letty was already having second thoughts.

"High school is over-rated. I'm so over all that childish stuff."

"Okay. Talk to your parents and let me know."

After Ashley left, Letty turned to Chloe. "What just happened?"

"It appears you've got your first protégé."

"Hah." Letty rolled her eyes at the suggestion.

"No, I mean it. You get Ashley into Juilliard and other dancers will come to you for instruction. You could become the primary source of advance training for serious dancers, a stepping stone to New York."

"You're teasing, right?"

"No, I'm not."

"There's a number of dance schools in Detroit."

"But none with the expertise you bring, at least none that I'm aware of."

"What about Joy's School of Dance?"

"You know as well as I do, most of our students won't go beyond the classes we offer. There's nothing wrong with that. Dance training will help them. It's good training for life. They walk with grace and greater confidence. But someone who is interested in dance as a profession, they need more than what we offer. You can be that next step. Think about it."

She was thinking about it, would think about it. But, was she the right person?

Chapter 36

Dale knew Ashley was up to something when he had given her the ultimatum on attending church. He just didn't expect to find out what so soon.

He was surprised to come home from work and have Ashley tell him and Ava she wanted to talk to them. Usually it was the other way around. Now he knew how Ashley must feel when he and Ava told her they wanted to talk to her.

"What's this about?" he asked. He and Ava were sitting together on the couch, their accustomed spot for such conversations.

"Dad, Ava, you know I've been working real hard, focusing on dance."

"Yes, we're proud of you and how hard you are working," Dale said.

"Well, you see, there's only so far I can go at the dance studio here in Cascade Falls."

"Where do you want to go with it?" Ava asked.

"I want to go to Juilliard, but I'll never be able to do that if I stay here."

"Wait. What are you talking about? Stay here? Where else would you go? You're only sixteen." Ava squeezed Dale's hand to calm him down. Only Ashley could get him worked up so easily, so quickly.

"That's just it. Letty says she could work with me, but not here in Cascade Falls."

"So we drive you to Detroit. It's not like we haven't done that before."

"This isn't once a week, Dad. I need to practice and work with her every day."

"No, out of the question. We'll arrange to take you to Detroit once or twice a week. The rest of the time you can take classes and teach at the dance studio here in Cascade Falls. You'll finish out high school here as well. What were you planning on doing about school?"

"I can take courses online to finish my degree. There's all kinds of opportunities online now. Not everyone is suited for a traditional high school setting."

"Is this about going to church with us? Because if it is, let's discuss that."

"No, it's not about that. It's about me, my life, my career goals, doing what I need to do to achieve them." Ava continued to hold his hand. Ashley was being unexpectedly calm and rational, not what he expected. That just made it worse. Instead, he was the one feeling irrational, ready to explode. He liked it better the other way, could handle the angry, teen-age Ashley better than this more mature Ashley.

"Have you talked to your aunt Sara about this?"

"Not yet, but you know she will say yes as long as you are okay with it."

"I'm not okay with it. This is a lot to take in. When would you propose to go to Detroit?"

"Once this semester is over. I'll finish up my classes before moving."

"That would be mid-January. I don't know. It's a lot to think about. We need some time to think it over and get back to you."

"Take all the time you need, as long as you decide before the semester is over so I can make arrangements." Who was this girl and what had she done with his daughter? Was it possible she was maturing?

He and Ava discussed it later that night, once the kids were upstairs in their rooms.

"What do you think? What should we do?" he started the conversation. He was surprised when he saw tears sliding down Ava's cheeks. She had been so calm earlier that day when Ashley had asked them about leaving.

"I always thought I would be a good mother if I ever had kids, but now I'm wondering."

"You are a good mother. You're the best mother that you can be. That's all any parent can do. Ashley is just one of those challenging kids."

"If I've been doing so well, why is she so intent on leaving?"

"Because she's Ashley. Besides, what kid doesn't want to leave home as soon as they can? Most of them would love to do what Ashley is proposing. They just don't have the goals and resources."

"It's more than that. Ashley, she never really accepted me. She has tolerated me, but that's all." Ava reached for a tissue. "If her mother were still alive, this conversation never would have happened."

"You don't know that. Ashley is just being Ashley. I don't think Joy would have handled things any differently. All kids rebel against their parents."

"I didn't."

"Then you were different. You and your mother had your difficulties, right?"

"Yes." Ava nodded her head. "Sometimes … sometimes I feel like I'm still living in Joy's shadow. It's a hard place to be."

"I'm sorry if I have contributed to that in any way."

"I know you don't mean to. You don't recognize it when it happens." Dale slid forward on the couch, holding her hands in his as he searched her face. What to say? What could he say?

"Do you love me as much as you loved her?"

"That's not a fair question." Dale slid back into his spot on the couch, dropping her hands, surprised by the question.

"I know, but I'm asking anyway. I know that I will always be in second place where Ashley is concerned and I'm okay with that. I'm not her mom, never expected to replace her mom. As long as I'm not second place with you."

"How can I compare you? Joy was my first love, my childhood sweetheart. There's so much we shared. I loved her more than I thought possible. After she died, I was numb inside. I didn't think I could ever love again." Dale turned back to face her. "Then you came along and I realized, I could love again. Did I love her more? No, I loved her differently. I love you both but in different ways. You are two different people."

"I guess that makes sense."

"Does it help?"

Ava nodded and wiped her tears.

"Ashley loves you in her own way," Dale continued. "Different from how she loved her mother, but not less. She would have rebelled against Joy just as she is rebelling against us. I know Joy would have been upset over Ashley's decision not to believe in God. I don't know what anyone of us could have done to prevent that."

"And I love her, too. That's why we have to let her go."

"Why?" Dale shook his head as he tried to comprehend.

"Because. I don't think this is just the words and actions of a rebellious teen. She has thought this out. She's old enough to decide for herself."

"At sixteen?"

"Yes, at sixteen. That's old enough to become an emancipated minor. Ashley is showing a maturity beyond her age group. Much though we may not like it, I think we need to let her go. If we don't, she might resent us and find a way to leave us anyway."

"So, is it black mail? If we don't let her go, she'll make life miserable for us?"

"No, that's not what Ashley said. There were no threats implied. It's just … reality. If we keep her from realizing her dreams, would she ever forgive us? Would we ever forgive ourselves?"

"I guess all that's left is to contact Sara and see if she's okay with it."

"And let Ashley know." They sat together on the couch in silence for a while longer before going upstairs.

Time enough tomorrow to start making the arrangements. For tonight he was going to enjoy having all three of his kids under his roof for however much time he had left.

Chapter 37

Ontario, Canada, 1853

Nathaniel was ferried across the Detroit River that night. He was welcomed by other escaped slaves and given a place to stay for the duration, whatever that would be.

Nathaniel had much to be thankful for and much to pray about when he went to church that Sunday at Sandwich First Baptist Church. He looked about him in wonder. This was no segregated church, but a church built by blacks for blacks. He didn't know such things existed. It was populated by escaped slaves and free blacks.

As he glanced about the sanctuary, he caught the gaze of a young woman sitting across the aisle from him, deep in song. She smiled briefly then continued to sing.

The preacher was in the middle of his sermon when bells started to peel and the choir struck up the song, "There's a Stranger at the Door." What a strange thing to do. Nathaniel had never heard of anything like it in his twenty-eight years. He felt himself grabbed and pushed to a trap door in the church's wooden floor. The young woman from across the aisle was beside him.

"Hurry," she said as she grabbed his arm and guided him down a dark tunnel.

"What?" Nathaniel asked.

"Shhh," she put her fingers on his lips as they heard the sound of boots stomping on the floor above. Nathaniel waited in the dark, musty corridor. He couldn't see who was waiting with him. He fought back a cough from the dust as the boots continued to tramp above. Close by he could hear the young woman's breathing. Finally, the boots stomped in the direction of the front door. They heard the door slam with a loud thump. Had they come for him? Had he put all of these good people in danger?

A light showed behind them at the end of the tunnel. He was pushed in the direction of the light, remaining silent lest the invaders were still close by. At the end of the tunnel was the church basement. Nathaniel breathed a sigh of relief as he came out into the light. With him was the young woman and the people she had been sitting with, another young woman, two older women and a boy.

"Bounty hunters," the young woman said before he could ask.

"I thought we free here," Nathaniel said.

"Trackers still cross the river from Detroit and capture escaped slaves," the woman explained.

"Then, no place safe?"

"When the bells ring and the choir starts the song, that means trackers have been sighted. The tunnel built to hide church members."

"No place safe?" Nathaniel asked again.

"No, I reckon not, not as long as slavery legal."

Nathaniel stayed for three months with the community in Ontario. During that time, he pondered what to do, where to go. He thought about going further into Canada where bounty hunters would be less likely to track him, but he missed Cascade Falls and the friends he had made there.

He also courted the young woman he had met that Sunday. When messengers from Cascade Falls finally found him and brought him the news of his freedom, he proposed, she accepted, and they planned for a new life together, back in Michigan.

Chapter 38

Letty visited her great aunt the week after Christmas once she got back to Detroit.

"I thought you were spending the holidays with us," her mother protested when Letty announced she was going home. Home, since when had Detroit started to feel like home? Maybe once she left?

"Sorry, Mom, but I've got a date for New Year's Eve. Have to be back for that. And, there's always work to be done when you are starting a non-profit. You know that."

Her mom smiled. "That I do." Letty appreciated that her mom made no further comment about her work and Freedom House.

She brought Aunt Letty a poinsettia and a bag of the peppermints she loved. She was pleased to see another poinsettia and a box of chocolates in her aunt's room, evidence that she had not been forgotten over Christmas.

"Did an admirer stop by?" Letty teased and pointed to the poinsettia and candy.

"Just that no good daughter of mine."

"No good, Aunt Letty? Why do you say that?"

"Because she only comes to visit when she wants something. I fooled her. My money is safe where no one can get it. And my good jewelry, that's locked up in a bank so no one can steal it. Not even you."

"Aunt Letty, why would you say that?"

"Why else would anyone come sneakin' round? Nobody wants to visit an old woman over the holidays."

"You know, that's why I visit. I'm just coming for the peppermints, which I bring."

"Hmmmph," her aunt said, refusing to be coaxed into a smile.

"Really, Aunt Letty. If that was how you treated me when I come to visit, I can't blame cousin Ella for not coming more frequently."

"Shut your yap. Did you bring me my peppermints?"

"Always."

"That's good 'cause that no-good daughter of mine, she doesn't know enough to bring them. Brought me these chocolates instead. Here, you take them." Her aunt handed her the box.

"I'm sure there are plenty of people here who would like a chocolate."

"Then you give them to them. My own daughter doesn't even know what her mother likes."

Letty could see it was going to be one of "those" days. How to coax her aunt out of her snit?

"Auntie, tell me about Christmas when you were little. Christmas with my grandmother."

"Not much to tell. We were poor, but not as bad off as some. We always had income from my daddy's barbershop and mamma took in laundry. Those were hard days, back then, during the depression. People didn't have money to spend on haircuts or laundry. I don't know how Mom and Dad got by till things got better, but they did."

"We've had a long line of barbers in our family."

"Have I ever told you about your great grandfather Nathaniel?"

"Many times."

"Did I tell you how the white folk in Cascade Falls bought him out of slavery?"

"No, Auntie, you didn't. How did it happen?"

"He'd been living in the poorhouse, working as a porter in a hotel. Word was that his owner came looking for him. That was six years after he had left. His master had a long memory and a long reach. The abolitionists got word about his owner seeking him out and snuck him out to Detroit where he crossed the river into Canada. The owner threatened a lawsuit against all those who helped him escape. The people got together and put up the money to buy him. Word was that they paid eight hundred dollars for him, for one slave! Sojourner Truth only cost twenty-two dollars. Barbers were worth money back then. Even in slavery your ancestors were higher class than those field slaves. And his wife, yours and my namesake, she was a seamstress. Another skilled trade."

"What are you saying, Aunt Letty? That our ancestors were better because they had more money?"

"That's right." Letty was surprised by her aunt's prejudice against other members of the same race.

"We also had ancestors who worked the fields," she reminded her aunt.

"None worth remembering."

"Remember how Great Grandma's family had a farm?"

"That's how we got through the depression. Grandma brought us eggs and fresh vegetables and potatoes or we would have nearly starved. But they owned their farm. They weren't slaves or sharecroppers." Letty chose not to argue the point. She understood why Aunt Letty's daughter and granddaughter came so infrequently. She wouldn't come herself, but not every visit was like this one, and she suspected, in her own begrudging way, that her aunt appreciated her visits.

"When are you bringing your children back to visit?" Aunt Letty asked. Letty had brought a group of students to the nursing home before Christmas to perform. Then they gave the residents small gifts they had made, paper Christmas baskets with homemade cookies and nut breads. Aunt Letty insisted on calling them her children.

"Maybe in the spring. The weather is so unpredictable in the winter."

"I'll be dead and gone by then."

"Don't say that, Aunt Letty. You're far too ornery to go without a fight."

"I didn't say I wouldn't fight, but this is one battle no one wins."

"What battle is that?"

"The dance with death."

Letty didn't correct her. "Well, I expect you'll put up a good fight and come spring, you'll still be here."

"Lord willing, not that my daughter would care." The conversation had come full circle, back to the hole of her own making, in which Letty had found her aunt.

"Come on, Aunt Letty. We're going for a ride." When all else fails, getting her aunt out of her room usually helped. She rolled her down the hall, stopping constantly as her aunt talked to other residents along the way.

"Where are you taking me?" Aunt Letty asked.

"Where do you want to go?"

"Anywhere but here."

"Then let's go on a magic journey. You take me back in time to your favorite Christmas. Can you tell me your favorite Christmas memory, Auntie?"

Letty saw tears form in her aunt's eyes, an unfamiliar sight, as she sought the words that gave justice to her memory. Letty took her to the lounge and sat her next to the Christmas tree.

"What is it, Auntie? I'm sorry if my question made you sad."

"Not sad, child. Blessed." Her aunt took Letty's hand in hers. "Blessed by too many good memories, memories long gone of Christmases gone by."

"Tell me one. Please, Auntie."

"When I was a little girl, one Christmas, my father, your great grandfather, he came in with tears in his eyes. My father never cried before and never cried since. He said, the pig, the one we were raising to butcher and feed our family for Christmas. It was gone, stolen. Some hobos that my mother had given some of our meager share of food had stolen him."

"That was going to be our Christmas dinner," her aunt said as a tear slid down her cheek.

"How is this a happy memory, Aunt Letty?"

"Because, when our neighbors heard about what happened they butchered their own pig and brought us over a ham and bacon. Their son brought it over. That was what folk did back then. We didn't have nothing, but what we had we shared. That boy, that was your Uncle Elmer, my first husband. He died in the war, World War II. He was my first and only love."

"Cousin Ella's father?"

"Yes."

"But I thought he died in the nineties."

"That was her stepfather. A mean-hearted man."

"Didn't you love him?"

"Not the way I loved Elmer. Maybe he knew that. But a girl with a small child to raise, she needed a husband. At least that's what my mamma said. So I married Jonas. He was a good man, but a hard man. A strict man. He hit my baby. There was nothing I could do about it."

"Did he hit you, too?"

"What could I do? I wasn't strong enough to leave him. I wasn't like my namesake."

"Great Grandmother Letty?"

"Yes. She was a strong woman. She escaped slavery then came back to Cascade Falls with her husband, back into the land of slavery. She raised five children. When her husband wanted to go fight in the Civil War, she didn't stop him. Not that she could have."

"I didn't know that Great Grandfather Nathaniel fought in the Civil War."

"Many Negros enlisted. They felt it was their duty to help free others. So Great Grandpa enlisted. He must have known Great Grandma Letty was strong enough to handle the hardship of his absence. But the war was over before he was called to serve. He died five years later, leaving her with five children to raise, but Great Grandma Letty, she was strong. She raised her children and never remarried. My grandmother used to tell me about her.

"You're stronger than you realize, she used to tell me. You have the blood of escaped slaves in your veins. Never forget that. And you, you never forget that either," her aunt admonished her. "You are stronger than you think you are. Now get me back to my room. I need my nap."

Letty never knew what to expect when she visited her aunt Letty. She wheeled her back and slipped out of her room, pleased by the backhanded compliment.

Chapter 39

Detroit – Present Day

Letty was surprised to find the heat on when she unlocked the door to Freedom House the day after New Year's. Had she mis-programmed the thermostat? She thought she had turned the heat down to fifty-five degrees over the Christmas break. It wasn't supposed to kick on to heat the building beyond that until classes started again next week.

She was even more surprised when Derrick greeted her from the top of the stairs.

"Hey, I didn't think you were coming back till next week," he said.

"Classes don't start till then, but I've got work to do to prepare for the next session."

"Great," Derrick practically ran down the stairs. "There's someone I want you to meet."

Letty didn't know what to say when Derrick introduced her to a family of three sitting in the kitchen.

"This is Asad and his wife and baby. They're from Syria."

Letty pulled him aside. "Derrick, what are you doing? I thought we were out of the refugee business after what happened last time," she whispered.

"Don't worry. They don't understand English. Asad only knows enough to get by. You can talk freely."

This didn't ease her worries at all.

"And what's more, the board isn't in support of this. What are you thinking? After what happened, don't you think ICE will be watching us? I don't want another incident like the last upsetting the students."

"Don't worry. This is different. Asad and his wife have green cards."

"I thought you had to have employment to get those?"

"They do have employment, here."

"Derrick. We can't afford to pay anyone. I'm not even getting paid."

"And that will change soon. We provide a place to live while Asad looks for a more permanent position."

"Can we do that?"

"As far as I know we can. And if it turns out we can't, we'll claim ignorance."

"You know ignorance of the law doesn't hold up in court." What was he thinking? Letty shook her head in disapproval.

"So sue me. Oh, wait, that may happen."

"Not funny, Derrick."

"It will be okay, Letty. Besides, what would Great Grandma Priscilla say?"

"She's your great grandmother, not mine."

"If you heard their story, you wouldn't question having them here. Besides, you yourself said it felt more like a home with a family living here." Letty had to agree with that. Still she was not going to allow herself to get attached to this family only to have them ripped away from her.

"I hope you know what you are doing," Letty said. "I've got work to do." She started to leave.

"Oh, one more thing." Derrick stopped her. "I know you haven't found a church yet. I thought maybe you'd like to try my church. It's right here in the neighborhood. Actually, I've only started to attend recently, but it feels like home. I thought you might like it."

"I'm sorry, Derrick. I told Walter I would go to church with him this Sunday."

"You're in luck. They have a Sunday evening service we can attend."

"I don't know."

"You're the one whose been talking about being more a part of the neighborhood. This is one way."

Derrick had her there. "Okay. Sunday night," she agreed. Derrick walked her to her office.

"You and Walter? You an item again?" he asked.

"We never were an item."

"You dating again?"

"Yes. He got the Pinedas out of detention and into jobs. It's the least I can do."

"Oh," Derrick shrugged his shoulders, "a duty date."

"Not a duty date."

"Then what is it."

"A date. Why can't it just be a date?" Letty shook her head again. This man was infuriating.

"A date is never just a date."

"What are you talking about? Maybe where you are concerned, but where I come from, a date can be just a date."

"You keep telling yourself that," Derrick said and went back downstairs to the kitchen.

New Year's Eve with Walter had been fun. Walter knew all of the best restaurants and night clubs in Detroit. They had ended atop the Renaissance Center watching fireworks.

She had spent New Year's Day with Sara and her family watching football. By the next day she was ready to get back to work. After her break she felt she had renewed energy and a renewed vision. She was going to work on getting the art gallery set up in preparation for a grand opening, maybe in February during Black History Month, or in spring when the weather was more predictable. She was going to bring up the proposal at her next board meeting.

Now here was Derrick, muddying that vision. Why did he have to be so exasperating? But how could she kick out a family with a small baby?

Chapter 40

Cascade Falls – Present Day

"Can I have Ashley's bedroom?" Jacob asked when they told him and Grace about Ashley moving to Detroit.

"No one is moving into Ashley's room. You both have your own bedrooms. Ashley will need a room when she comes home," Dale told him.

The weeks of January passed more quickly than he ever remembered. Usually the cold month dragged by. He found himself hoping something would come up to change Ashley's mind, something to keep her from moving out. But Ashley remained firm in her resolve to move to Detroit.

Life with Ashley had improved since the agreement to let her move. She was more considerate of her brother and sister, as well as Ava and him. She was happier and more talkative, no longer the taciturn teen. Mostly she talked about Juilliard. It seemed she had explored every aspect of its website and had even contacted Juilliard for further information.

"Did you know they have an option where you can finish your last year of high school while attending? I put in my application but it may be too late. Only problem is that you don't qualify for federal financial aid. Do you think we could afford it?" Ashley stated at dinner one night.

"You already applied? When was this?"

"In December. I just thought I would try. Didn't think it was an actual possibility till I talked to Letty."

"When were you going to tell us? Didn't you need our signatures on the application?"

"I forged them." Nothing Ashley did surprised him. "And paid for it with my own money." What next?

"You know, I could become an emancipated minor. That way I would qualify for financial aid based on my own income," Ashley continued. "Juilliard doesn't allow ballet students to work while attending because of the physical demands of the program. That means I'll have to be able to pay everything or take out a lot of loans since I won't be able to earn any money myself while attending."

"Emancipated minor?" Dale asked.

"Yes. It means I'm living on my own, supporting myself. That's pretty much what I'll be doing once I move to Detroit."

Again, Dale looked at Ava. Punch to his gut. Where is Ashley getting all of this? And what happened to his little girl? Since when did she become an adult with an adult goal? Where had her childhood gone? Even as she talked, he hoped something, anything, would happen to cause her to change her mind.

"It's not a reflection on you, Dad, if I do. I know Juilliard is expensive. I'm trying to make it as easy on you as possible."

By ripping my heart out? "We'll look into it. We have to think about it." Dale looked across the table at Ava. It would be hard to pay her way at Juilliard. His business was doing well and they had Ava's salary as well, though she didn't make as much at St. Luke's as she would at a public school. He doubted Ashley would qualify for financial aid based on their income. And he had Jacob and Grace to consider, though Ashley would probably be graduated by the time Jacob was ready for college — that is if he went to college, which was questionable at this point.

"There is a summer intensive program I could attend, but I can't do that if I'm to start classes in the fall. If I don't get in for next fall, maybe I could do that." Ashley continued to chatter about Juilliard, oblivious to how he was feeling.

He wondered what Joy would have thought about Ashley's intent to attend Juilliard. She probably would have supported her, been just as excited as Ashley, leaving him alone in his opposition. He wondered what Ava was thinking. He knew they would talk later that night. He also knew, having already told Ashley she could move to Detroit and apply for Juilliard, Ava would say they could find a way to pay for it. Again, he prayed that something, anything, would happen to keep his little girl home. But that would mean crushing her dreams.

No, they would find a way.

Chapter 41

Detroit – Present Day

Letty took a deep breathe before entering her great aunt's room with Derrick. He wanted to meet her, wanted to hear her stories first hand. The problem was, would she want to meet him? You never knew where Aunt Letty was concerned. Maybe today would be a good day.

"Auntie," Letty came in and gave her a hug and kissed her on the cheek.

"Who are you now?"

"Your niece, your favorite niece," so far, not so good.

"Just fooling you. I know you. And who is this young man?" Her great aunt's face broke into a smile, pleased with her cleverness.

"Ha ha, Auntie. This is Derrick, a friend."

"Pleased to meet you, Aunt Letty," Derrick carefully extended his hand. "Letty has told me so much about you."

"What you doing, dating a white boy?" Aunt Letty ignored Derrick's outstretched hand and spoke directly to Letty as if Derrick weren't there. "Is this what your great grandparents suffered for, so you could betray your own race, date a white boy?"

"Auntie, he's not my boyfriend. He's just a friend."

Derrick feigned insult at this, "Just a friend? Like an old sock you can use and throw away?"

Letty whispered to him. "You know what I mean. Don't make this any worse than it is."

"Don't worry. I'm good with old people."

Letty groaned at this. She would see. Derrick's social skills were not his strength. He proceeded to talk to Aunt Letty.

"Much as I would be honored to call your beautiful niece my girlfriend, that's not the case."

"Why not? My niece not good enough for you?" Not helping, Letty thought but refrained from interfering.

"I'm the one who's not good enough for your niece. She won't have me. Besides, she has another beau, one more deserving. I, on the other hand, am available. What about you?"

"Don't try to play me, young man. I've been played by far better than you. I'm no one's fool, but you can give me a little sugar." Aunt Letty pointed to her right cheek. Derrick gave her a polite peck.

"That's what I'm saying," Aunt Letty responded with a smile. "The old girl still has it."

"That she has," Derrick said.

Letty was surprised at the turn of events. Leave it to Derrick to find a way around her great aunt.

"Auntie, Derrick thinks his ancestors and our ancestors may have something in common," Letty said.

"And what would that be?"

"His several times great grandmother Priscilla was an abolitionist. She owned the house where I have my dance studio … remember, Freedom House?"

"I remember some such nonsense about the place you work."

"Do you think any of our ancestors may have passed through the house?" Letty asked.

"Possible. Nathaniel stayed somewhere in Detroit before passing over to Canada."

"My great grandma's records don't include any names. It would have been too dangerous for her and her guests. I'd like to find out more about the people who passed through Freedom House. Anything you remember would help," Derrick said.

"All I know is that it was a large house in Detroit. There was a room in the basement to hide slaves. My grandmother said something about a kind woman in Detroit that Great Grandfather Nathaniel had contact with. After the war, whenever he had business in Detroit, he would visit her, even stay overnight."

"Does the name Priscilla Jacobson sound familiar?" Derrick asked.

"Don't know. Hard to remember."

"Is there anything else you remember?" Letty asked.

"Some talk about a governor. It was a joke between the missus and her servants."

"Governor?" Derrick and Letty exchanged glances. Grandma Priscilla's son had run for governor. Maybe the old woman's memory was on target.

"Something about someone running for governor. But I know how to find out."

"How, Auntie?" Letty asked.

Her aunt rolled her wheelchair over to the dresser that held the TV. She reached for the bottom drawer and pulled out a notebook. "Here it is. All of my grandmother's notes about our ancestors."

"Aunt Letty, you never told me you had this," Letty exclaimed.

"You never asked me. How else do you think I remembered all those things I told you." Aunt Letty handed the notebook to her. Letty flipped through the carefully organized sheets.

"This is wonderful."

"Maybe if I visited that house of yours, I could remember more."

"Auntie, would you like to visit? You never said anything about wanting to."

"You never asked me."

"That can be arranged," Derrick stated.

"I'll check with the social worker, but I think so," Letty agreed.

"Good. Now you go on. I have to get my beauty rest. But don't forget to bring your friend back next time." Aunt Letty dismissed them.

"That went surprisingly well," Letty commented on the drive home. "Aunt Letty doesn't usually take to visitors."

"What can I say?" Derrick said. "I'm good with old people and kids." That you are, Letty thought. An odd duck, but he had his good side.

Chapter 42

Detroit – Present Day

Derrick had been right about his church. Those in attendance were a hodge-podge of homeless, immigrant families, students and social activists. Letty had been uncertain at first. The service was different from her AME roots and the hymns lacked the vibrancy of the full gospel choir at Walter's church, but what they lacked in vibrancy, they made up for in sincerity. There was off-key singing, but everyone participated, singing with the voices God gave them. Gospel music was accompanied by guitar and drums. The clatter offended her trained ear at first, until she listened with her heart. The preacher spoke to her, messages that addressed the inequities in a city of extremes — extreme poverty and extreme riches as Detroit sought a comeback and money was poured into regentrification and renewing old buildings.

Afterwards there was a potluck with a variety of smells and tastes Letty hadn't experienced since coming back to Michigan. Immigrant families prepared dishes from their home country. There was plantain, peanut sauce, Thai noodles, recipes from Africa, Asia and Latin America. Letty was embarrassed by the abundance of riches in this impoverished congregation. What did she have to offer?

"Derrick, why didn't you tell me about the potluck? I would have brought something."

"You can make up for it the next time."

"Presuming there will be a next time," Letty smiled.

"I haven't met your friend yet." The minister approached them. He had a heavy African accent. Derrick explained he came from South Africa. That explained his English. South Africans spoke far better, more proper, English than American English with all of its slang. He had married a white woman he met while she was serving as a missionary in South Africa. They had married and eventually decided to move back to her home state of Michigan where they set up this church.

Both he and his wife warmly welcomed her. How could she not come back?

"You belong there," Derrick said to her on the drive home.

"Why do you say that?"

"Because you've got a heart as big as Montana."

Letty broke out with laughter at this. "Have you even been to Montana?"

"For your information, I have. I haven't lived my whole life in Detroit. I moved to Montana to study architecture."

"Why Montana?"

"Because Montana, with its wide-open spaces, seemed as different to Michigan with its lakes, hills and forests as possible. I needed a change."

"Then what brought you back?"

"I missed Michigan's lakes, hills and forests." He shrugged his shoulders. "You can get lost in Montana's big sky and never even know you are lost."

"Just as you can get lost in Michigan woods."

"Oh, no. Michigan woods are unique, each one of them."

"And so are you, Derrick Jacobson."

"I take that as a compliment."

"Take it however you want." Letty continued to smile at the conversation. Was he flirting? She didn't think he knew how.

"And I meant it as a compliment."

"What?"

"The reference to Montana. You have a heart for the homeless, the hurting, the lost. I meant it as a compliment."

"Oh, thank you." What else could she say? She was taken aback by his sincerity. This man was full of surprises. "I did like your church." And if Derrick was right about this church, what else might he be right about?

Chapter 43

Detroit – Present Day

This board meeting had gone so much better than the one in December. The board agreed with having a spring open house. They didn't think they would be ready by February, but did want to do something for Black History Month. Letty planned to have her history of the Underground Railroad operation at the house ready in time for that as well as some dances. She was putting together a brochure with an abbreviated history to give out to everyone who attended.

She was limited in what she could do because of the age of her students. There is only so much you can do with pre-school and Kindergarten through second-grade students. Ashley proved to be a boon in this regard. Not only was she a help with the younger students, she quickly learned dances Letty knew from Alvin Ailey and was ready to perform both with her and solo. Ashley lived and breathed dance that first month as she got ready for her audition for Juilliard. She had missed the February audition date in Chicago, but was scheduled for the last audition in March in New York. Letty would have liked more time, but was doing what she could. Between that and her online course work, Ashley didn't have time to do much of anything else.

Sara did a series of charcoal sketches to illustrate the history Letty was composing. They were displayed in the ballroom. Light refreshments and punch would be served and of course, donations solicited at the end of the performance.

Letty arranged to have her great aunt come to the Black History Month celebration. Derrick picked her up and helped her in and out of his car, stowing her wheelchair in his trunk. They didn't have an elevator for her wheelchair. But they did have a chair lift on the steps to the second floor, so with assistance, she was able to watch the dancers. She was in her glory. She brought her bag of peppermints with her and handed them out to the young dancers. Letty watched out of the corner of her eye. Derrick kept her aunt entertained since she was busy with the open house and performances.

Afterwards she introduced Walter to Aunt Letty.

"Aunt Letty, this is my friend, Walter."

Her aunt looked him up and down. "What is it you do, young man?"

"I'm a lawyer."

She shook her head in approval. "He'll do."

"Do what?" Walter asked.

"Don't ask," Letty told him. She left Walter with her great aunt and Derrick as she mingled among the guests.

Dale and Ava came with Jacob, Grace and Grace's friend Josie.

"We've been studying about the Underground Railroad in school," Grace told her. "Did you know Josie's home was once part of the railroad?"

"That so? My family members first came to Cascade Falls by way of the Underground Railroad. Maybe they stayed in your home."

"Oh, I just know they did. Don't you think so, Josie?"

"My grandmother says lots of slaves passed through our home back then, before the Civil War," Josie said.

"Then maybe they did. We'll have to compare notes sometime. Maybe the next time I'm home."

"That would be great," Josie said.

Letty felt a light tap on her shoulder.

"Letty, what you've done for Ashley," Dale started. "I may not be the best judge, but I can see how much she has improved since she has started working with you. Thank you."

"Thank you for letting her work with me. She is quite talented." Letty had been pleased as well by the progress Ashley had made in a short amount of time. She looked over at Ashley who was holding court among the other dancers. She had improved, but was it enough?

Chapter 44

Cascade Falls – Present Day

Kathleen wasn't sure about being called Grandma. Surely, she was too young for that. But one thing she was sure about, she was head-over-heels, to-the-moon-and-back, crazy in love with this baby boy. She couldn't get enough of rocking him, walking him, burping him, even changing his diaper. It was all wondrous. And it was a good thing because Stephanie seemed far from interested in the care of her son. Kathleen loved caring for her grandson, but she was beginning to worry when after three weeks, Stephanie still showed little interest in her baby. She had thought by now the utter exhaustion from childbirth would have lessened and Stephanie would have more energy to take care of him, especially once the holidays were over and she was needed back at the Center.

Kathleen left the baby with his mother, then found them in pretty much the same position when she got home, Stephanie stretched out on the couch, holding the baby.

"Here," she gladly relinquished him as soon as Kathleen came in the door. "He needs a diaper change."

"Let me get my coat off," Kathleen told her, threw off her coat, then picked up the baby.

"He's hungry, too," Stephanie said. She had made a feeble attempt at breast feeding while in the hospital. When he didn't latch on right away, she gave up and opted for a bottle.

Just as well, Kathleen thought. Easier for others to help with his care. She wondered if that had been Stephanie's plan all along.

If Stephanie knew who the father was, she wasn't letting on.

"At the least he could help you with child support," Joe told her when it came time to fill out legal papers.

"No. I don't want anything from him," Stephanie insisted. "I don't want him in my life or my baby's life."

"What's the baby's name?" everyone kept asking, but Stephanie refused to give the baby a name.

"You can't take him home from the hospital until you give him a name," Joe told her.

"I don't know, Dad. You name him."

"How about Joseph?" Kathleen suggested. When Stephanie frowned at the prospect, Joe came up with another option.

"I think one Joe is enough. Do you want to name him after his dad?" Stephanie glared at her father. "Just checking. How about naming him after my grandfather, Augustus Aloysius Michaels?"

"I like that," Kathleen said. "What do you think, Stephanie?"

When Stephanie didn't appear to hate the name, it was decided.

"Augustus Aloysius," Kathleen said, rocking the baby in her arms. "Or Gus, for short." And so, the baby was named. They set up a nursery in Grandpop's old room with a bed for Stephanie as well, keeping the other upstairs bedroom for when Josh or Michelle came home.

"Is this lack of interest in her own baby a common thing?" Kathleen asked Joe.

"No, not that I'm aware of. It's normal to be exhausted but most of the new mothers I know are ecstatic, if exhausted. They relish the time they have with their babies. That's how Stephanie's mother had been. What about you?"

"I'm not sure I remember. It's all this haze. I know I was tired. I also know that I really wasn't ready for a baby. I was happy to hand the baby over to my mom."

Joe tried to talk to Stephanie about it the next day, but she refused to talk. Josh was more excited about his nephew than Stephanie was about her son. He came home every time he had a day off from work.

"If you think he's so great, you try feeding him, cleaning spit-up out of your hair and changing his dirty diaper," Stephanie said. Josh was happy to do each of these tasks, which set Stephanie off into a crying spell.

"Am I really such a bad mother? Everybody is better with my baby than I am."

Kathleen talked to her ob-gyn about it. "It just doesn't seem right."

"Sound like post-partum depression. What does her doctor say?"

"She hasn't seen her doctor since the baby has been born. He's in Kalamazoo. She doesn't have a local doctor."

"What about the baby? Isn't he due for a check-up?"

"We set up an appointment with a local pediatrician. Would you see Stephanie?"

"I don't like to take another doctor's patients away."

"Please, she needs to see someone." Kathleen's doctor agreed, as long as Stephanie was willing to come, which she wasn't.

"I have my own doctor in Kalamazoo. I don't need to see your doctor."

"We're just concerned, Stephie," Joe told her. "You don't seem to be yourself."

"If I'm such a burden, then I'll pack up my stuff and Gus and we will be on our way."

Kathleen felt her heart jump into her throat at the thought of Gus leaving. "You're no burden, Stephanie. You and Gus can stay here as long as you want. We're just worried about you. In fact, if you want to get rid of your apartment and move in with us, you can." Kathleen didn't look at Joe as she said this. They hadn't discussed any such thing, but the thought of Stephanie moving out and taking Gus led her to make the offer.

"No, that's okay. I need to be getting back to work soon. No maternity leave in retail. I've been getting calls asking when I was coming back."

"So quit. I'm sure you can get a job here," Kathleen said.

"And stay in Cascade Falls permanently? No way."

"But how will you take care of Gus while you work?"

"I'll find childcare, like every other single mom I know."

Stephanie seemed determined to leave after that, till she wasn't. Kathleen found her collapsed on the couch again each day. She thought better of saying anything and risk losing little Gus.

The back and forth continued for three months, with Stephanie saying she was leaving but never taking the steps necessary to leave.

Then one day, that changed. Kathleen came home for lunch as had become her custom so she could check on Gus and help Stephanie. Stephanie was up and dressed and waiting for her.

"I've got a job interview. Can you watch Gus?"

"Today? Right now? Where? In Cascade Falls?"

"No, Kalamazoo. Will you watch Gus?"

"Of course. I'll just call Chloe and let her know I won't be back."

"Good. And afterwards I'm meeting some friends so I won't be home for dinner."

"That's fine, Stephanie. Just watch the roads."

"Duh, Kathleen. I've lived in Michigan all my life. I know about winter weather. I'll see you later tonight."

When it started to get late and there was a snow advisory, Joe received a call from Stephanie saying she was staying over in Kalamazoo at her apartment because of the weather.

"Okay, honey. Stay safe. We'll see you tomorrow."

Kathleen was waiting for Stephanie when she got back the next morning.

"How was it? Did you get the job?"

"I did." Kathleen's heart sunk at the words. She knew the time with Gus was not likely to go on forever, but still ... "I need to talk to you and Dad about it. But mostly you."

"What about?" Kathleen held Gus tight as Stephanie spoke.

"It's just ... It's a great opportunity. They want me to start right away. But I don't have anyone to watch Gus."

"We'll watch Gus for you until you work out childcare."

"That's just it, Kathleen. About Gus. I'm really not much of a mother. You're so much better at this than I am. I was wondering if maybe you and Dad would take care of Gus for me."

"For how long?"

"Until I get back on my feet?"

"How long might that be?"

"I don't know, Kathleen. I'm really not ready to be a mother. You used to talk about having a second chance at being a mother. Well, maybe this is it."

"Are you saying you're abandoning Gus?"

"No, not that at all. I'm leaving him in his grandparents' care. That's not the same thing."

"I have to talk to your father about this."

"I know, but I need to know right away."

"I have to talk to your father about this," Kathleen repeated.

When Joe came home, she pulled him into the kitchen before he could go into the living room and see Stephanie and Gus.

"I take it Stephanie is back."

"Oh, she's back all right."

"What does that mean?"

"It means she has a new job and wants us to take care of Gus for her."

"For how long?" Kathleen saw the wrinkles around his eyes seem to sag as he took in what she said. Kathleen knew that look. It was his sad, resigned look. It seemed that look was never far away when dealing with Stephanie. She wanted to wipe it away. Assure him it was okay, but it wasn't.

"That's what I asked. She couldn't say. Joe, I think Stephanie is planning on running off, leaving Gus for us to raise."

"Are you sure"

"No, but she indicated as much. Keeps talking about how she's not cut out for motherhood. What should we do?"

"What do you want to do? This could be the answer to our prayers for a baby. A backward way of getting an answer from God. God does write straight with crooked lines." Joe was surprisingly calm at the prospect. Kathleen wasn't sure what she thought. She sat down and looked at her hands.

"Don't you think I've been asking myself that? I couldn't love that baby more than if he were ours. But …" Joe pulled up a chair next to here. "Oh, Joe, I did want a baby, do want a baby. But not like this. I've been thinking about it all day. Thinking how much I would like to raise Gus as our own. But I don't think that would be fair to Stephanie. I don't think she knows what she's doing. Can we really let her do something she may regret for the rest of her life? The way I regret leaving Josh and Scott?"

"This is Stephanie. If she's made up her mind, I don't think there is anything we can do to change it. We have to do what's best for Gus."

"But what is that? Is he better off with his mother or us? I know my boys were better off with my mom back then, but Stephanie is different. This is different."

They talked and prayed before talking to Stephanie.

"Stephanie," Joe started. "Kathleen told me about your job opportunity and about watching Gus for you. We are just wondering, do you really know what you are doing?"

"Dad, I know. I'm not a kid."

"No, you're a grown woman with grown-up responsibilities."

"It's just that …" Kathleen added, "some decisions once made, there's no going back. This time you have with your baby is precious. It's gone before you know it. Are you willing to give that up?"

"You gave that up and your sons came out just fine."

"Yes, but I've regretted that. For years I've regretted all I missed."

"And now's your chance to get those years back by raising Gus."

"That's not how it works. I just don't want you to make the same mistakes I made." Kathleen approached Stephanie. She didn't know whether she wanted to hug her or shake her.

"It's my choice. Look, if you don't want to take care of Gus, I can find someone who will." Kathleen's heart ached at the thought. Of course she would take care of Gus.

"No, not at all. We'll take care of Gus. But who's going to take care of you?" She reached out to hug Stephanie then backed off, aware how unwelcome that hug was. "We just want you to think about what you are doing."

"Don't you think I have? It's all I've been thinking about for the past three months. I'm going back to Kalamazoo. If you won't help me, I'll take Gus and find someone who will." She started to pick up the sleeping baby from bassinet.

"Don't do that." Joe stopped her with a light touch of his hand. "Of course, we'll take care of Gus if that's what you want. He's our grandson."

"That's what I want."

So it was settled, Kathleen thought. Gus woke with a loud cry. Without stopping to think, Kathleen picked up her grandson and shushed him. Holding this baby felt so natural, so right. Why did her stomach feel so unsettled?

Chapter 45

Detroit to New York – Present Day

Ashley loved living with Aunt Sara. She was way cooler than her dad and stepmom and was an artist. Ashley didn't even mind having her pesky cousins around. They gave her the adulation she deserved, unlike Jacob and Grace. Life was good. Away from family and family obligations like church, she now had the freedom to focus entirely on dance. Her mornings were filled with study and completing her high school coursework. In the afternoon she went to Freedom House with Letty, practiced and then later taught afterschool classes.

The only negative was Caleb. She missed him. They had facetime most nights, when she was back from the dance studio and he was done with practice, homework and work. They both were too busy to hang out together. So what if she was now almost a two-hour drive away? No, life was good, she reminded herself.

Ashley had the date of her audition in red on the calendar of her cell phone, eagerly marking off the days. She was glad neither her dad or Ava were coming. She needed to focus. Letty was accompanying her. She would understand. Aunt Sara was also coming. She was going to talk to some people about her art. She would also understand.

When she boarded the flight to New York, an unfamiliar feeling hit her. Could this be anxiety over the audition? Strange. She didn't like this. Butterflies in her stomach, keeping her from eating, words racing through her mind. She couldn't rest. She wished she was dancing. When she was dancing, everything faded away. It was just her and the music. Dance required a concentration that didn't allow for distraction. She loved the discipline. This other, it was all new for her. She had always exuded confidence as befitted someone with her ability. Dare she allow the thought? Was it possible she would not pass the audition? Impossible. It couldn't happen, so no need to think about it. But what if?

"Doing okay?" Letty asked as Ashley stared out of the window of the plane.

"Why wouldn't I be?"

"Just asking. I know I'm always nervous before an audition. It's normal."

"I'm fine. I'm fine. Stop asking."

Ashley was relieved when Letty didn't say anything more. There was nothing she could say, nothing anyone could say.

"This time tomorrow it will be over," Aunt Sara said.

"Don't say that. It sounds so final."

"The audition will be over. Then the next adventure begins, whatever that might be," her aunt explained.

"I'm just focused on the audition." Ashley continued to stare out the window.

Letty had tickets for an Alvin Ailey performance that first night.

"Better than sitting in a hotel room worrying," she told Ashley.

"Who's worried?" Ashley insisted.

Letty figured it would help take Ashley's mind off of the audition, whether Ashley wanted to admit she was worried or not.

Afterwards, she took Sara and Ashley backstage to meet some of her friends. She introduced Ashley as her "protégé", smiling as she did so. Imagine her, having a protégé.

"Are you a dancer too?" one of the troupe asked Sara.

"No, but thanks for the compliment." Letty continued to smile as she heard this. Sara had always been self-conscious about her weight. Having someone suggest she was a dancer was praise Sara deserved to hear.

"I'm an artist," Sara stated.

Letty laughed as she joined in the conversation. It felt good to be back with her New York family, felt natural. It was good to be away from the stresses of Detroit and starting a dance studio. She hadn't felt so light since she moved away.

"You coming to the club?" Shaunte asked.

"Not tonight. Ashley has a big day tomorrow. She's auditioning for Juilliard."

"She is a protégé then." Shaunte gave Ashley a high five. "Good luck on your audition."

Ashley smiled despite herself.

"Come out tomorrow and we can celebrate," Shaunte said, then took Letty aside. "You know, we still have openings. Are you ever coming back from your leave of absence? Do you want me to talk to Adelaide?"

"That's not what this trip is about. It's about Ashley."

"Still, would it hurt? Have you been keeping up your training?"

"Yes," Letty didn't want to admit it, but now that she was back, she couldn't believe she had ever left.

"Do you want to spend your youth training others to dance, or dancing yourself?"

Good question. Letty didn't have an answer.

The audition started at ten. Ashley breezed through the ballet and modern technique classes, as Letty knew she would. By the time of her solo performance Ashley was back to her confident self. Letty waited around during the auditions, hanging around the Lincoln Center. Sara was meeting with art dealers while she stayed to support Ashley. Family and friends weren't allowed to watch the audition, so she was relegated to waiting. If all went well, the audition would take all day. If not, Ashley could be dismissed at any time during the process. She needed to stay close by in case that happened. It felt good to be back at the Lincoln Center. She stretched her legs and went out for some fresh air.

"Leticia." Letty turned at the sound of her name. Adelaide.

"I heard you were in town."

"Did Shaunte tell you?"

"Actually, I found out through my connections at Juilliard. I hear you have an impressive student auditioning."

"That I do."

"Have you any more of them?"

"Not yet, but I hope to."

"I hope you will keep us in mind as an option for your students."

"Of course."

"Unless," Adelaide slowed down. "Unless you're interested in coming back. We can't keep your place open forever." Letty could feel Adelaide peering at her. Adelaide kept her face non-committal. "Have to make sure you haven't gotten flabby in your time away." Adelaide seemed content with what she saw. "Call me. You know the number," she said before breezing away as was her custom.

Chapter 46

New York – Present Day

She was crushing this, Ashley thought as she made it through the coaching session. The ballet and modern technique classes in the morning had been easy. She performed the solo she had done for the Black History open house and was invited back for the coaching session. The purpose of this session was to see how quickly she could pick up the choreography for a new routine, how well she took direction and worked with others. She picked up the dance steps quickly, though struggled some with fitting in with the other dancers. She was more used to solo dancing than dancing as part of an ensemble. But she had done well enough to be called back for an interview, the final hurdle to jump.

"Do you know what they might ask?" Ashley asked Letty.

"Just be yourself. They are looking to get to know you better, who you are outside of dance. What your interests are, your goals, whether you are ready to undertake this course of study."

"I'm ready."

"I know you are. You just have to let them know that. You'll be fine," Letty told her. Ashley didn't believe her. She had practiced for everything but this. Tell her to dance, she could. Ask her questions … Aunt Sara joined them.

"How is it going?" she asked.

"Good. Ashley made it to the final round."

Aunt Sara hugged her. "I knew you would. What's next?"

"Interview," Letty said as Ashley heard her name called. She was ready for this, she told herself.

Ashley fielded the first questions with ease. She was beginning to believe she could do this.

"What if you aren't accepted into Juilliard?" What was this woman saying? How could she not be accepted? Until this weekend, the thought had never crossed her mind. What would she do?

"I guess I haven't thought beyond today's audition. If I don't get in?" Ashley asked.

"Yes, what will you do?"

"I guess I'll try again next year. I don't know. Maybe apply for the summer session. Why? Are you saying …?"

"You are young. Are you truly ready? This will be an extremely rigorous environment. You won't have time for a social life. I see, you are planning on completing high school online. You'll be missing out on all the high school activities, prom, graduation parties. Are you really ready to give up all of that?"

"I've been working for this all my life. I just didn't know this was what I wanted until a year ago. If I thought I wasn't ready, would I be here? Would I have moved to Detroit to work with Leticia? I've already given up high school activities. I'm ready."

The woman made some notes on a tablet in front of her as Ashley waited. Should she say more? Had she said enough?

"That will be all," another one of the interviewers said. Was it all? Her fate was being decided.

Letty and Aunt Sara were waiting as she knew they would.

"How'd it go?" Letty asked.

"Fine. It went fine. Can we go now?"

"Chloe told me, after every audition, she would go out, have some fun, and forget about it. How about it?" Aunt Sara asked.

"No, I'd rather just go back to the hotel."

"Whatever you want," Aunt Sara said, but Ashley saw the look she gave Letty. She didn't care. All she wanted was to go back to their room and to go home tomorrow.

Dale was surprised to see Ashley's number come up on his phone. "Ashley," he told Ava before answering.

"Ashley. How did it go? We've been thinking about you all day."

"Daddy?" Dale heard Ashley's voice crack. Another gut punch. What could be wrong with his baby?

"What's wrong? Didn't it go well?"

"It went well. I made it through to the final interview."

"That's great. Then what's wrong?"

"I want to come home."

"You are coming home, tomorrow."

"No, I want to come home to Cascade Falls."

"You know you can do that any time. Your room is here for you. What's wrong?" If only he could see her face. This did not sound like his Ashley.

"What if I made a mistake?"

"Did you learn something?"

"Yes, I guess."

"If you learned something, how can it be a mistake?"

"What if this whole Julliard thing, leaving high school, my friends. What if that was a mistake?"

"You can always come back. I'm sure you can get back into school. If anything, you'll be beyond your class. If that's what you want." Dale couldn't let himself get his hopes up. After all, this was Ashley.

"I don't know what I want. I'm just afraid I made a mistake."

"You know, Ashley, this isn't like Irish Step Dancing when you chose not to compete in the Internationals."

"Are you saying this is not my choice?"

"No, I'm saying, this is something you've been working very hard at. A goal you set for yourself. Not like step dancing that you did for fun. It's your choice, but not one to be taken lightly. Some choices have greater consequences. Once made, you can't go back."

"You mean, if I get accepted into Juilliard I can't quit?"

"No, you can always quit if it's not right for you. But if you are accepted and turn down the opportunity, another might not come along. This is your chance to follow your dream, or not. You are free to choose. And you are free to make a mistake."

"Sometimes freedom isn't all it's made out to be."

"Sometimes, Ashley. Come home tomorrow. I'll pick you up and we'll talk about it, okay?"

"I just wanted to hear your voice."

"Any time, you know that. You can always call."

"I'll be fine. Love you."

"Love you too," Dale said as he ended the call.

"Is she all right? What happened?" Ava had been sitting next to him, trying to fill in the blanks of the conversation.

"I don't know. I'm not sure what's going on. She said she wanted to hear my voice." What was up with that kid? "… She was talking about coming home."

"That's good."

"I guess. With Ashley I never know." He sighed and continued to look at his phone. Did he dare call her again? Or would she push him away?

Ashley had wanted to call Caleb but she knew he had a basketball game that night. Not a good time to call. Instead she called her dad and sent Caleb a text.

"miss u. text me."

When the phone rang shortly after hanging up with her dad, she thought it was him.

"Dad, I'm okay," she said before looking at the number.

"What's up?"

"Caleb?"

"Yeah. You texted me. How did it go today?"

"Don't you have a game?"

"I do but it hasn't started yet. I figured if it was important enough for you to text me on a game night, it was important enough for a phone call."

"It is, but it can wait until after the game."

"You sure?"

"Sure. Call me when you get home."

"Some of us are going out after the game. It may be late."

"Okay. Call me tomorrow."

"Are you sure you're all right?'

"Sure. I'm fine. Just remember to call me tomorrow." Of course he would be going out after the game. Why wouldn't he? All the things you are supposed to do when you are in high school. She wouldn't blame him if he started dating someone else. They weren't exclusive. He better not.

Here she was, sitting in a hotel room in New York. Was it really worth it? She had neglected all of her friends in order to focus on dance. The only friend she had left was Caleb. How much longer would he hang around? He probably is dating other girls, will probably ask them to the prom. Meanwhile she sits in this hotel room. She should have taken Letty's offer to go out. But no, she'd rather be by herself.

Aunt Sara came back shortly after this with the salad she had requested.

"You sure you don't want to go out? It is New York. We can walk along Times Square. Maybe it's not too late to get cheap seats for a show."

"That's okay, Aunt Sara. You go. I don't want you to miss out."

"I'm not going without you. Come on, let's spend some of your dad's money." Aunt Sara pulled out the credit card Ashley's dad had given her before they left.

"Wasn't that supposed to be for emergencies?"

"And this isn't an emergency? Your dad wouldn't want you to mope in your hotel room."

"Okay," Ashley agreed. Aunt Sara was right. Dad wouldn't want her to mope alone in her room. Besides, Caleb wasn't exactly sitting home alone. Why should she?

Chapter 47

Cascade Falls, 1853

Nathaniel had left Cascade Falls in the dark of night, hidden on a wagon. When he returned three months later, it was daylight and he was riding atop a wagon, with his wife by his side and their means of making a living tucked securely in a pack by his other side. Nathaniel had tried to arrive quietly, but word got out quickly that a precious cargo was arriving that day. The same farmers who had left their fields three months ago, came back to be part of his welcome back. They shook his hand in welcome, patted him on the back and welcomed his wife as well.

When the hub-bub had settled down, the first person Nathaniel wanted to see was Josiah Whitcomb. He went to Whitcomb's office, knocked on the door and let himself in when invited. Josiah jumped up to greet him, smiled and shook his hand.

"Welcome home," he said. "And who is this?" he asked when he saw Letty hanging back.

"This my wife, Leticia Wright," Nathaniel announced with pride.

"Nathaniel, you come back, not only a free man, but a married man as well. Congratulations," Josiah said.

"About that, my freedom. I plan to pay back the people who bought my freedom."

"Now, Nathaniel, the money is already spent and gone. No need to pay it back."

"I want to pay it back. Once I earn the money. I want you to arrange it."

"How are you going to do that?"

"As a barber. I open a shop as soon as I find a place. And my wife, she a skilled seamstress."

"The best way to pay us back is by doing what you are preparing to do. Be a successful businessman and an asset to our community. When the opportunity arises, maybe you can help someone else."

"That I will, sir. I want you as my first customer. Any time you need a shave and a haircut, you see me, no charge."

"I will do that, but not for free. You've provided enough free labor during your life. From now on you will be working for yourself." Josiah turned to Letty. "And I will let my wife know about your services. I am sure she can get you some business."

Nathaniel and Letty took a room in the poorhouse until able to rent a room. Nathaniel rented a space in a local saloon and quickly began to gain a reputation as a barber.

Before moving to Cascade Falls they had discussed their options.

"There already plenty of barbers and seamstresses in Detroit. A smaller place might offer more opportunity," Nathaniel had said. And so they had decided on Cascade Falls. They were going to save enough money to buy Letty's freedom eventually, but they figured she was as safe in Cascade Falls with her new name as she was waiting on the border of Canada. And once they were settled and had a place of their own, they arranged for Letty's mother, brother and Sarai to come and stay with them. Letty's sister had married a man in Canada and stayed behind.

Finally, a home, a family, and a business. Nathaniel believed his good fortune. He had known as a young man, that someday he would be free. Someday he would be somebody, and now he was.

Chapter 48

Cascade Falls – Present Day

Kathleen woke up when she heard Gus cry. Joe slept through it. She figured she needed to get used to waking up and feeding him for when Stephanie leaves. She heard light footsteps and the sound of shushing while Stephanie warmed up a bottle. They put two bottles in a cooler in the room each night for night time feeding. Then the bottle was placed in a bottle warmer. It saved going up and down the stairs with a crying baby. Modern conveniences. Didn't have them when Josh and Scott were babies. She remembered getting up with crying babies, heading for the kitchen. She hadn't breast-fed her babies either. She remembered nights sitting in a rocking chair and crying as she fed the baby. She had been so tired. Better get ready to do that again, she told herself.

Some nights her mother would join her and take over so she could sleep. What had she been thinking? How could she have left those tiny perfect beings? Yes, she had left them in capable hands but … for all the terrible things she had done in her life, this was what she regretted the most. She just hadn't been thinking, hadn't realized what she was doing. How could she get Stephanie to think, really think about what she was doing?

Kathleen thought she heard the sound of stifled sobs coming out of the nursery. She climbed out of bed, pulled on a robe and knocked gently on the nursery door.

"Stephanie? Are you all right?" When she didn't get an answer, she quietly opened the door. Stephanie was sitting in the dark in the rocking chair, feeding Gus and crying.

"Stephanie? What's wrong?"

"Nothing," Stephanie said through tears.

"I know something is wrong. Do you want me to get your dad?"

"No," Stephanie said with such emphasis that the bottle almost came out of Gus's mouth, waking him momentarily. "No," Stephanie said much quieter. "He wouldn't understand."

"Try me."

"Kathleen, I've made such a mess out of my life. Who am I to think I can be responsible for another human being?"

"None of us are perfect. Look at me."

"You're okay."

"Really? That's quite a compliment coming from you." Kathleen hoped she would get a laugh out of Stephanie from this. Instead she got more tears.

"I just don't know what to do. How can I leave him? But how can I raise a child alone?"

"You're not alone. You have me and your dad."

"Not if I move back to Kalamazoo."

"You'll have Josh then." The sleeping baby spit up formula round the nipple of the bottle. Kathleen handed Stephanie a cloth to wipe up the milky white spittle.

"I can't even feed him right."

"You're doing fine. I think he needs to be burped." Stephanie carefully lifted Gus to her shoulder and rubbed his back.

"How important is that job to you?" Kathleen asked.

"It's everything."

"Everything? Really, Stephanie?" Kathleen pulled up a chair and sat down next to her.

"It's everything I want. Better pay, though longer hours. More responsibility. I would be floor supervisor."

"You can't find a position like that here?"

"Maybe eventually. First, I would have to be hired. No one hires after Christmas. Then I would have to work long enough to be noticed, be considered for a raise. I also have school to think about. I want to finish my degree. How can I do that, work full-time, and take care of a baby?"

"It's a challenge. Some have done it, but I don't know how."

"I know I can't do it."

"But can you really give him up?"

"It won't be forever."

"You say that now, but then the years go by and your children are growing up not knowing you."

"I'm not you."

"I know you're not. It seems you are stuck in either or thinking. Either you go to Kalamazoo and leave Gus with us, or you stay here and feel trapped, like you'll never get out of Cascade Falls. I know that kind of thinking."

"I do feel trapped, not just at the thought of staying here, but by Gus. I feel so guilty about that. How can I consider my baby as my jailer?"

"It all depends on how you look at it."

"How?"

"I spent years in prison. I was physically trapped. I fought it for a long time, but one day I realized, it was only a trap if I chose to let it be a trap. I started studying, planning for my future. When I stopped fighting the system, I started using the system. Slowly, my life got better."

"How did you figure that out?"

"I'd like to say I did it on my own, but actually it was some nuns, in prison for civil disobedience, who taught me that. They said, prison isn't a prison when you freely choose it. They felt freer behind prison bars than out in freedom. They felt they were making a difference by being there. That made all the difference. I didn't entirely understand it, but it worked. Just a change in perception."

"I don't get it."

"I didn't either, at first. Over time it started to make sense to me. You can fight motherhood and all the responsibility that's part of it, or you can embrace it, freely accept it for what it is. It's all up to you, all how you look at it."

"I don't want to be trapped."

"You don't have to be. I know it can feel like a prison right now. You can't go where you want to go, do what you want to do without first thinking about Gus. But if this is something you freely choose, it will start to feel less like a trap and more like an opportunity, an opportunity for so much love. And you don't have to give up everything just because you're a mother."

"You're saying there are other options?" Stephanie turned her head and looked at Gus who had fallen asleep on her shoulder. She rubbed his back and gently leaned her head against him.

"There are always other options. You could look for work here while you take care of Gus and go to school part-time. You have a place with us and built in babysitters for Gus. Then, when and if you are ready to move somewhere else, you do it from a position of strength, not desperation. You'll have your master's degree and more work experience and Gus will be older and easier to place in day care."

"You make it sound easy."

"It won't be easy. But the easy way isn't always the best way. I took the easy way when I left my boys with my mom. Now I have a lifetime of regret. Would it have been hard to raise them? Yes. I would have had to change my lifestyle, something I wasn't willing to do back then. I grew up eventually. You're older than I was in terms of maturity."

"Really? You think I'm mature?"

"More mature than I was at your age. The bar isn't set too high." Kathleen reached over, removed the spit-up cloth and tucked the blanket up around Gus's neck. "I think Gus is back to sleep, and I need my sleep too. And so do you. One of the first rules of new motherhood, sleep when you can because you don't know when you'll get the chance again."

"I think I'll take my chances." Stephanie closed her eyes and continued to rock Gus.

Kathleen took one last look at mother and child then quietly shut the door.

Chapter 49

Ashley stared at the envelope in her hand. Her heart fluttered in an unfamiliar fashion. There it was again. That same feeling she had experienced before her audition. Could it be self-doubt? She didn't like it.

"Are you going to open it?" Aunt Sara watched as Ashley rubbed the envelope between her fingers.

"I don't know. It seems wrong to open it without Letty."

"Then let's get her." Aunt Sara was out the door and across the lawn before Ashley had a chance to respond. Was it possible Aunt Sara was more excited about this than she was? Was it possible that here in her hands was the answer to her dreams or the crushing of her hopes? Somehow it seemed wrong that something as ordinary as an envelope could contain such monumental news. Ashley lagged behind her aunt, slowly making her way up the stairs to Letty's garage apartment. Aunt Sara was already in Letty's apartment delivering the news.

"This is what we've been waiting for," Letty said as she walked in.

"I know." Still she didn't open the envelope.

"What are you waiting for, Ashley?" Aunt Sara asked.

"You open it." Ashley handed the envelope to Letty. "It's as much about you as me."

"Not really." Letty took the envelope. "But if this is what it takes to get you to open this …" She slipped a finger under the sealed edge of the envelope, ripping the envelope when it refused to cooperate and release its contents.

Ashley watched as Letty read the letter, her face showing no indication of what the contents held. Letty glanced over the letter once more before raising her head with a smile. "You're in."

"I'm in?" Ashley questioned.

"You're in," Aunt Sara repeated.

Ashley stood silent, her feet frozen to the floor.

"What's wrong?" Letty asked. "Aren't you excited?"

"I … I don't know." Ashley fumbled for words. In the pit of her stomach, something ached. Sorrow washed over her and she felt tears spill out where there should have been excitement. What was wrong with her? "I wish my mom were here."

"Oh, Ashley. She would have been so proud of you," Aunt Sara said.

"I know. I still miss her."

"She's here, in your heart." Her aunt pointed at Ashley's chest.

"That's not enough." Ashley faced her aunt. "Aunt Sara, is this how it is going to be my whole life? Will every important event be ruined because my mom can't be here to experience it with me?"

Now it was her aunt's turn to fumble for words. "Ashley, I don't know. I miss your mom too. You can be sad and happy at the same time."

"I guess so, because that's how I am right now."

"The fact that you miss her is a testimonial to how much you loved her, still love her. Would you rather not miss her?"

"No, I guess not. Will this ever get easier?"

Aunt Sara glanced at Letty. When Letty didn't come to her rescue, Aunt Sara said what she could. This confirmed it, no one knew how she felt.

"I'm sorry, Ashley. This isn't my area of expertise. Maybe your Uncle Joe …"

"I don't want to talk to Pastor Joe. You're okay, Aunt Sara. You remind me of my mom. It's like having her here. I'm glad you are here to share this with me even though my mom isn't." Ashley wiped her eyes. "So, what now?" she asked Letty.

"We send them your acceptance and start planning for fall, unless," Letty paused and tilted her head, "you are having second thoughts."

"Duh, no. It's Juilliard. Of course I'm going." Ashley hugged Letty and allowed the excitement she had blocked to slide through. "I have to call Caleb and let him know." Ashley said as she pulled away from Letty. "And Dad."

She rushed down the stairs, her feet carrying her lightly over each step.

Chapter 50

Detroit – Present Day

Letty watched Ashley depart and laughed. "Wow, talk about flip-flop. I don't know when I've seen anyone change moods as quickly as Ashley."

"Teens," Sara answered. "Now that Ashley is all set, where does that leave you?"

"What are you talking about?"

"I mean, Ashley knows what she's going to be doing for the foreseeable future. What about you?"

Letty knew what she meant. She just didn't want to answer.

"Look, Letty. I know you took a leave of absence from Alvin Ailey to help us get Freedom House up and running. We're not on firm ground yet, but …" Sara paused. Letty suspected Sara didn't want to bring up the unspoken possibility any more than she did. "If you want to go back to New York, back to Alvin Ailey, you are free to do so. You don't owe us anything. You've already done more in the nine months that you've been here than we expected. We just need you to finish out the year. That will give us time to look for the right person to replace you."

Replace her? Why did it hurt so much to hear those words? Would it be so easy to replace her? No one is irreplaceable. They will replace her at Alvin Ailey if she doesn't come back, and she'll be replaced at Freedom House if she leaves. It's her free choice, freedom earned by the blood of her ancestors. Why was it so hard to choose?

"You know, Sara, all my life, I grew up in a black, middle-class family. I went to predominantly white schools, all of my friends were white, but I never totally fit in. I didn't fit in anywhere. Not with my white classmates, or with my cousins who weren't middle class, whose parents scraped by to make a living.

"It's like there was a bigger gap between me and my cousins than between me and my white friends. I think that's why I studied social work in college. Why I wanted to provide programs for those who couldn't afford them. To prove myself. I've been living in two different worlds, and I don't fit in either of them.

"Then I went to Alvin Ailey. I met other dancers who were like me. Black dancers who celebrated their history through dance."

"I'm happy for you," Sara told her. "If you want to go back, I understand."

"No, you don't understand. I didn't entirely fit in there either. It was good for a time, but there's more to life than dance. There's Making a difference, having a purpose."

"We've talked about this. Letty, whatever you do, you will make difference. You can't help but make a difference. It's just you. You've got a heart as big as Montana." Both women broke out laughing at this. Letty had told Sara about what Derrick had said months ago. It had become a running joke for them.

"You know, Letty, there's no right or wrong answer here. Sometimes those are the hardest choices. No matter what you choose, you will be having an impact. Whether a dancer on stage, telling your story and showing other young girls what they can do, or as a dance instructor, teaching what you have learned."

"And someday they will surpass me, like Ashley already has."

"It's your choice, Letty. A choice only you can make."

My choice, Letty thought. Why is this so hard?

Chapter 51

"Come with me," Ashley told Caleb. Between her trips home and his trips to Detroit, they had managed to maintain their relationship. That would change once she moved to New York in the fall. They met at the park in Cascade Falls, where Ashley and Caleb had first met, years ago.

"I can't move to New York. You know that," Caleb responded.

"No, I don't know that. Come with me."

"What would I do there?"

"There are plenty of colleges in New York. You could apply."

"And what about high school?"

"Okay, move there, finish high school and establish residency, then go to college."

"I can't do that. I'm not you. What does New York have for me?"

"Me." Ashley reached out and took both of his hands in hers, gazing directly into his eyes. How could he not see this? How could he not come with her? Caleb shook his head.

"Ashley, you'll be so busy with classes. You won't have time for me, won't have time to miss me."

"You really think that?"

"I know that. I know you. You are the most driven, committed person I know. If you decide you are going to do something, you will. You go to New York, dance in the American Ballet Company, follow your dreams."

"What about you?"

"My life is here, at least for now. I don't know what I'm going to do. I just know I'm not ready to leave yet. I'm going to finish my senior year here in Cascade Falls. Maybe go to college somewhere in

Michigan. I don't know. I do know, I would just be in your way if I went to New York."

Ashley wanted to protest, but she knew he was right. She didn't want anyone or anything to get in her way once in Juilliard.

"Does that mean we're breaking up?" she asked.

"Were we ever together? You never let me give you a ring. Said you didn't want to be tied down."

"I guess."

"Here," Caleb pulled his class ring off of his finger. "I want you to have this."

"But we're breaking up."

"Yes. I want you to have this to remember me. I never was big on rings anyway."

"Are you sure?"

"Ashley Reese, when have I ever said anything I didn't mean?"

"Like always."

"This I mean. Take it." Caleb pressed the ring into her hand. Ashley clasped it tight.

"I don't have anything to give you."

"That's okay. Someday, maybe I'll come to New York and see you dance."

"You don't like ballet."

"But I like you," Caleb said as he squeezed the hand with the ring. Ashley unclenched her hand and looked at the ring, trying it on her fingers. Didn't fit.

"I'll keep it for you. Someday, I'll give it back." She put it into her pocket.

"You do that." Caleb smiled, pushed her hair back and kissed her. Ashley squeezed the ring in her pocket. She would remember him.

Chapter 52

Cascade Falls – October 1853

Letty looked over the horizon as the wagon pulled to the top of the hill. She placed her hand on Nathaniel's, indicating she wanted to stop and take in the view. Nathaniel told the driver to stop for a moment. The long trip by wagon had given her lots of time to think about the events of the past few months. She wanted, needed, to take a breath before starting her new life.

With each arrival of slaves from Michigan, her mother searched the group, longing for news of her husband. After six years, Letty thought her mother would have given up. But no, her mother still held out hope that he would join them someday. This latest arrival seemed no different than the rest to Letty, but not to her ma.

Suddenly, Letty's mother looked intently at one of the arrivals, a spark of recognition in her eyes. "Thomas!" she cried.

Letty's mother ran to greet the man, welcoming him. She invited him to stay with them. "Thomas, he from massa's plantation," her ma explained as they prepared food for him.

"More tea?" her ma asked as she cleared away his empty plate.

"Thank you kindly," Thomas replied. Her ma refilled his tin cup with tea then sat down across from him. Her mother waited, afraid to ask that which she most wanted to know. Thomas glanced away, not meeting her gaze.

"Thomas," her ma started.

"No, Hannah. You don't wanna know." Thomas continued to avert his eyes.

"But I need to know." She reached for his hand and waited for him to look up. "Thomas, what happened? I need to know what happened to my William."

"He dead." Her ma let out a slight gasp and let go of his hand.

"How it happen?" she asked. "Tell me, Thomas," she added when he looked away again.

"The massa, he angry. He say he goin' make example of your William. It not enough to kill him. He hung him by his hands and whipped him where everyone see. He left him hangin' there three days. At night, we sneak him food and water. Every day more beatings, till finally the massa say he done with him, let him down. We try take him home, tend his wounds but the massa, he say, 'Hang him. Let that be a lesson to them.' Then he ride away."

Thomas began to cry, tears sliding down his dark face. He didn't bother to wipe them away.

"I sorry, Hannah. There nothin' to do. The massa, him sitting so high and mighty on his pretty horse." Letty saw a vein on Thomas' forehead pulse as he talked about the massa through gritted teeth. "The overseer, he tie the rope 'round William's neck and leave him hangin' from a tree. He leave him there hangin'. He set up a guard so we cain't cut him down, not till the massa say cut him down." Thomas stared passed her ma at the wall as he remembered.

"That night, we kill that pretty horse the massa so proud of, me and Ceasar. We snuck into the barn. Killed her fast, merciful, not like the massa killed William. It not the horse's fault. The massa never find out. No one tell him who done it." Her ma sobbed as Thomas finished his story.

"I sorry, Hannah, for bringin' you pain," Thomas said.

"No, Thomas." Sarai wrapped her arm around Hannah's shoulder and held her as she cried. "She need to know. Thank you, Thomas." That was the second time Letty saw her ma cry.

Letty stared at the panorama before her. Had it been six years since she had been here? Didn't seem possible. Now she was back, a married woman, married to a free man. She was ready for a new start.

The town looked the same as she remembered it from her perch in the hay loft. They had spent a week hiding back then. Through the window in the hay loft, Letty had been able to see the town below. Her mother had continued to resist all offers to stay in the farm house.

"We don't want to be trapped in no white woman's house," she had explained to Letty and Abigail.

When the threat of danger lifted, the man wanted to celebrate with a dinner, inviting others to share the meal with them. "We want to appropriately welcome our guests," he had said. But her mother would have none of it. Letty remembered the events of the previous week, back in Indiana.

The white folk in Indiana had been so happy to have them. They had given them a welcome reception, inviting other white folk and other escaped slaves. They were celebrating their escape to freedom. A table had been set outside with pies and desserts brought from the local farms. It wasn't the abundance Letty had seen at times at the plantation when the owner had hosted parties. Letty knew because she had been called upon to help prepare the food and serve the dinner. No, it wasn't as rich, but it was better. Good home cooking.

"Freedom fare," her father had called it. "Everything tastes better in the north. Tastes better when you free," he had joked with the man sitting next to him.

Then there was the sound of dogs howling and three men on horses came over a hill. People jumped up, chairs were overturned, food was spilled or left uneaten on plates. Daddy stood in front of them, coming between them and the men, giving them time to get away, but not enough time for him to escape. Letty glanced back. Her feet froze to the ground as she saw ropes tied about her father, pulling him after the horses. A scream was suspended in her throat, choking her, too powerful to express with a mere sound. Her mother grabbed her and pulled her forward, aided by Sarai. The white folk formed a barrier between them and the bounty hunters, helping them to the house. When they reached safety, Sarai hugged her mother as she cried. That was the only time Letty saw her mother cry, until that day in Ontario. Sarai became part of their family in that moment. They had watched from an upstairs window as her daddy was led away.

"I rather my children be dead than ever risk being taken back to slavery," her mother had told the farmer, the memory of what had happened just weeks ago in Indiana still fresh. "We leave tonight, by foot if necessary." Letty had seen her mother's clenched jaw and fixed eyes. She knew there would be no budging her. The man must have realized this as well. He agreed to hitch the wagon and send them on their way that night. What a price her mother had paid for their freedom. What a price they had all paid.

That had been six years ago. Now she was back. Back in Michigan. She breathed in the fresh, cool air. Autumn odors of frost and fallen leaves filled her nostrils as she gazed across the horizon.

Letty took her hand off of her husband's. He nodded to the driver to continue. They were coming home. Coming to their new home— Cascade Falls.

Chapter 53

Cascade Falls – Present Day

Dale couldn't believe this day had come. Ashley had been accepted into Juilliard for the fall. She had managed to complete her requirements for high school through courses online.

"It helped that I didn't have to take any religion classes," Ashley had commented one weekend when she was home. She had worked intensely on her dance routine for the audition. She had impressed them not just with her dance, but her determination, how she had moved to Detroit to focus on dance. Her essay had focused on her years of dance, first under her mother's tutelage. She was doing this both for herself and for her mother, she had written. It hadn't always been her dream. She wrote of her struggles accepting the loss of her mother and her resistance to accepting that dance was her call in life. Dale had teared up when he read it.

It had been hard enough moving her to Detroit. Then the whole family had come and had dinner with Sara and her family.

"Remember, it's an easy trip on Amtrak from Detroit to Cascade Falls. You come home anytime you want. I'll buy the ticket. Or I'll come get you," he had told her before leaving. But New York, that was a world away. What would he do in New York? It was like a foreign country. Would he even begin to know how to get around? Joy had gone to New York when she was young. She loved it. One time she had talked him into coming to New York and attending a performance at Lincoln Center. It had been okay. He liked Lincoln Center, but New York had been crowded, noisy and dirty. He didn't like the traffic or the subway. He had been happy to get home. He had visited Juilliard that summer with Ashley, but that trip had been enough for him.

The family had gathered the night before for a farewell barbeque for Ashley. Kathleen and Joe brought baby Gus, watching him while Stephanie was at class. His step dad, Peter, had helped him flip burgers and dogs. Peter had finally lost that additional twenty pounds. At forty pounds lighter, he was a new man. His gut no longer hung over his belt and he walked like he was twenty years younger.

"And, I get to eat red meat," Peter said as he put cheese slices on the burgers.

"In moderation," his mother added as she walked up with a plate of buns.

"Yes, dear," he winked at Dale. "That heart attack, best thing that could have happened to me. My wake-up call. That and your mother," Peter added as his mom poked him in the ribs.

"Don't you forget it." His mom laughed as Peter placed burgers into buns.

"And don't you forget us," his mom had told Ashley before they left. "I know New York is so big and exciting. Don't forget where you came from."

"Never, Grandma," Ashley had said and forgotten as soon as she said it. Dale could tell. How could Cascade Falls compare with New York? She was already gone before even leaving.

Jacob and Grace were oblivious to their sister's leaving, each lost in their own world. They gave their sister the required hug before she left. Nothing more.

Ava was going to help Ashley get settled. He dropped them both off at Detroit Metro airport. No sense in going inside. With security he wouldn't have been able to wait with them for their plane. Easier to drop them off rather than parking, lugging suitcases through the walkway to the terminal and down the escalator. This was easier on everyone. No long goodbyes. Just a quick kiss and hug at the car before driving away. Easier for whom? Nothing was ever easy where Ashley was concerned.

"Call me when you get there," he told Ava. At least he could count on Ava to call him.

He had been preparing for this all of Ashley's life, preparing for the day she would leave, sometimes with anticipation, those days when she had been temperamental and argumentative. He just hadn't expected it to happen so soon. Hadn't expected her to go so far away. She didn't even look back as she rolled her luggage through the doors of the terminal, leaving him to hold back tears as he climbed back into his car and drove away. Being prepared didn't make it easier.

As he drove, he noticed a text message on his phone. From Ashley. He pressed listen on the car dashboard to hear it.

"Thank you, Dad. Love you," was all it said.

It was enough.

Chapter 54

Detroit – Present Day

Letty looked at the transformed building. Just a year ago she had been wading through debris in order to make her way through the building. Now she was greeted by a gallery of artwork lining the walls of the former living room, a small museum and offices. The third floor, former bedrooms, had been turned into studios for starving artists. The second floor housed the dance studio.

Besides the dance classes she was offering in the ballroom upstairs and at local schools, she was training young students for careers as dancers, preparing them for auditions with Juilliard, Alvin Ailey, and other dance schools. She had even hired an assistant to help her with her booming business.

As she walked into her office she saw a bouquet of red roses, mixed with greens and baby's breath with a note from Walter. "Congratulations on the start of another amazing year of dance!" She smiled to herself as she read the note and smelled the flowers. Walter was proving to be an attentive and caring suitor, so different from James. So different from what she had expected when they had first met. It was … comfortable. Comfort is good.

She attended Sunday morning services with Walter and Sunday evening services at the church Derrick had found for her. Still so much to do, so many needs in this city. She was doing what she loved and also making a difference. The money she made from the advanced students helped fund classes for students from the neighborhood who wouldn't ordinarily be able to afford dance classes.

It had been a good year, a year full of challenges, yes, but she was starting to feel at home here in this city. Ashley, her first serious student, had sent in her acceptance to Juilliard and Letty had informed Alvin Ailey that she wasn't coming back to New York. Each set out on their own paths: Ashley off to a new adventure, Letty to take root in a place and with a people. The lure of New York remained but it was no longer a siren song in her heart, pulling her back, making her doubt her choices. It was a memory, a tune playing in the background of her brain, but one she could turn off when she wanted.

She had it all, she thought as she sat down at her desk and opened her computer. Dance, students, meaning and purpose.

She heard a noise outside her office and stepped out to investigate. Derrick was escorting another family through the house.

"Derrick, what's going on?"

"Letty, this is Mr. and Mrs. Baswir, from Indonesia."

"What about Emil and his family?"

"They have their own place."

"Oh, I see," Letty paused. Another new immigrant family. Dare she ask? Did she really want to know? "Carry on." She returned to her office.

Derrick continued to be Derrick. A pin in her side, poking her, pricking her in ways she didn't expect. Every few months he showed up with another family to live in the former servant quarters. Sometimes it was better not knowing.

"You want to grab lunch?" Derrick came back to her office. Letty looked at the flowers from Walter and back at Derrick. It was good to have choices, even if just for where to go to lunch. She was enjoying the freedom her ancestors had bought for her with their lives.

"Sure. Why not?" She closed her computer and joined Derrick as they chose from the array of local fare. They could go to any of the many different ethnic restaurants in town: Asian, Ethiopian, Indonesian, Mediterranean, Sushi, burgers, pizza. The city had it all—and so did she.

Discussion Questions

1. G.K. Chesterton said, "The moment we have a fixed heart, we have a free hand." How does this apply to the characters in *Freedom Dance*? How does it apply to your life?

2. Throughout her life, Letty struggled to fit in and find a place where she belonged. What has been your experience with trying to fit in? Have you had the experience of coming back to a place you had once belonged only to realize you no longer fit in? How did you deal with it? How did you find a home and belonging?

3. Kathleen struggles with understanding the gift of free will. Joe tells her, "if we didn't have free will, we wouldn't be able to freely choose to love God. What value is love if not freely given?" Have you struggled to understand why God has given us free will? What is your understanding of free will?

4. Slaves traveling on the Underground Railroad risked everything for freedom. What are you willing to risk for freedom? What price have you paid in order to be free?

5. This is a story of merging a past with the present. How important is history in contemporary society? How has history influenced contemporary times?

6. The number of "nones" in America (people who check "none" on surveys of religious affiliation) has been on the rise, especially among millennials (those born between 1980 and 1996). This includes atheists, agnostics and those who have no religious affiliation. What do you think is bringing about this change? Ashley decides she is an atheist. Have you had a family member or friend make a similar decision? How do you deal with such a decision?

ACKNOWLEDGMENTS

I owe a debt of gratitude to Linda Haas for her extensive research on the Underground Railroad in Jackson County, Michigan, where I have resided for the past thirty years and which is the basis for the city of Cascade Falls. Her presentation on her research at the Jackson District Library inspired me to include the Underground Railroad in this novel. Her book, *Michigan's Crossroads to Freedom*, provides significant research to support that the Underground Railroad operated in Jackson County, an often unrecognized and unacknowledged fact since the purpose of the railroad was to move freedom seekers quietly across the country with no fanfare or recognition for those doing the moving. Her book tells the stories of the safe houses along the way and the courageous abolitionists who provided shelter for those in need.

Her second book, *Hidden in Plain Sight*, provides the stories of the freedom seekers, slaves that escaped and risked their lives to find safety and a new life in the north. Her books provided me with the research and insights into this era in history which I needed to write Nathaniel and Letty's stories. Some of their stories are rooted in facts detailed in her books, others are pure fiction, made up as the stories and characters grew in my mind.

Her research resulted in a Michigan Historical Marker commemorating these events at Mt. Evergreen Cemetery in Jackson, MI, a significant accomplishment as each fact noted on the marker needs to be historically accurate. Stated on the marker: "Emma Nichols, a freedom seeker who fled from a plantation in Virginia and achieved her freedom through the secret network, is buried in this cemetery. She lived on Biddle Street in Jackson with her husband Richard Nichols, a barber who had also attained freedom through the Underground Railroad."

For information on the Underground Railroad, I encourage you to read her books. Another resource is *Slave Narratives: A Folk History of Slavery in the United States From Interviews with Former Slaves, Florida Narrative*, an online resource through the Guttenberg Project. This is an important part of our history and needs to be remembered.

Thank you to Linda Haas and all those historians committed to keeping the memory of these heroic individuals alive.

Note to the Reader

Did you enjoy reading this book? If so, please leave a review. Your comments would be appreciated and mean so much to me in terms of helping others notice my book. You, the reader, have the power to make or break a book in this day of emarketing and social media.

Thank you so much for reading *Freedom Dance*. Stay tuned for the next book in the series!

Patricia M. Robertson

Other Novels by Patricia M. Robertson

Dreamweavers – Dream again, wherever you are in your life.

Buying Time – Visit the peace movement during the Cold War era of Ronald Regan, SDI (Strategic Defense Initiative) and MAD (Mutually Assured Destruction).

Land of Deep Waters - Honduras, land of deep waters, a country torn apart by civil unrest, violence and poverty: Is it possible to go back?

Magnificent Failure - Is it possible to start over? Failures in the eyes of the world and their own eyes, Diane and Jake found each other.

Dancing Through Life Series

Dancing on a High Wire – What do you do when life knocks you off balance? Join Sara, Joy and Esther as each seeks to find a "new normal" and regain their balance on this high wire we call life.

Still! Dancing - Some phone calls we love, others we hate, like the ones Pastor Joe receives from his daughter's school. Or the one Dale received at work, letting him know his wife, Joy, had fallen and was in route to the hospital by ambulance. Could her cancer be back?

A Slow Waltz - The road to healing from loss is a slow one, sometimes going backward and sideways before going forward. Sometimes the biggest barrier to healing lies within us. Join Dale, Kathleen, Ava and others as they journey to forgiveness and healing.

An Irish Slip Step -The Irish slip jig is set in 9/8 signature time, unusual and a little off balance, like life! Kathleen didn't know about the slip jig, but she knew about slipping up. As did Chloe's, whose life was knocked off balance by an unplanned pregnancy. And then there was that fiery red-head, Mary Helen, who fell in love with an

American soldier. Was it a slip-step or one of life's fortuitous missteps that brought them precisely where they were meant to be?

Delicious Secrets - Pastor Joe's church secretary retired a year ago. Since then he has struggled to find the right person to fill this position. Enter Marcie, a twenty-something college dropout, trying to find her way in the world. A church secretary was the last job she would have chosen, but she makes the best of it by entertaining herself with real and imagined secrets about church members, until she stumbles upon a secret she would rather not know. Once known, there was no turning back.

Beautiful Questions - Some questions are so big, they can take a lifetime to answer. They are big enough for you to live in, walk around in them, taste them, touch them, and test them. These are not to be taken lightly. They are beautiful questions. What are the beautiful questions in your life? Join Gwen and others as they ask beautiful questions.

Lyrical Dance - All of her life Esther has taken care of others. How can she let others take care of her? Will she ever be herself again?

Meanwhile, Kathleen struggles to understand what it is to be a pastor's wife. Who is she now that she's married? Is it possible to grieve over the loss of a dream she didn't even know she had?

About the Author

Patricia M. Robertson is an author, speaker and spiritual director, who is committed to helping individuals find God in their every day experience. She also is author of a companion non-fiction book to *Still Dancing, Walking with Families through the Dying Process*, as well as *Walking with Families through Grief,* a companion to *A Slow Waltz*.

She has written other non-fiction books and writes a weekly blog and monthly newsletter. She has a Doctor of Ministry and over thirty-five years of experience in ministry to families. She currently is enjoying her own love story with her husband, Jack, grown children and grandchildren. For more information about her ministry, go to www.patriciamrobertson.com.

Man of the Month – Coming in 2020

The last place Gwen wanted to do her internship was her home town, Cascade Falls. But her father's heart attack and recuperation required her presence. So here she was, back at St. Luke's. Would she ever escape this place?

Meanwhile Gwen's mother recruits her friends to join her in the "Man of the Month Club." Their goal? To find an eligible young man every month for Gwen to date until she finds Mr. Right and settles down in Cascade Falls.

What could go wrong?

Will Gwen be able to survive her internship and escape Cascade Falls without a ring on her finger?

Join Gwen and other friends from Cascade Falls as she endures multiple disastrous first dates in book nine in the Dancing through Life Series.